# Rumour Has It

MAUREEN CHILD

First published in Great Britain 2013
by Mills & Boon, an imprint of Harlequin (UK) Limited.
Large Print edition 2013
Harlequin (UK) Limited,
Eton House, 18-24 Paradise Road,
Richmond, Surrey TW9 1SR



Special thanks and acknowledgement
to Maureen Child for her contribution to
*Texas Cattleman's Club: The Missing Mogul* miniseries.

ISBN: 978 0 263 23795 5

Harlequin (UK) policy is to use papers that are natural, renewable and recyclable products and made from wood grown in sustainable forests. The logging and manufacturing process conform to the legal environmental regulations of the country of origin.

Printed and bound in Great Britain
by CPI Antony Rowe, Chippenham, Wiltshire

**Amanda Would Not Be Scared Off By A Big, Gorgeous Sheriff With Eyes As Cold As A Winter Wind.**

"If you think you're worrying me, you're wrong," she said.

Nathan stared at her. "I don't want you worried. I don't want you at all."

Direct hit, she thought as an icy fist slammed into her chest and squeezed her heart. But she wouldn't let him see it. "I don't want you, either, Nathan. I'm not that young girl anymore, dazzled because Nathan Battle noticed her—"

He grabbed her, yanked her close and kissed her with a fierce desperation that was fueled by desire and anger, all twisted up together. She could feel it in him as she felt it in herself. Past and present tangled together and memories were as thick as honey on a winter morning.

But those memories were swamped by all of the new sensations coursing through her.

## *MAUREEN CHILD*

writes for Mills & Boon Desire and can't imagine a better job. Being able to indulge your love for romance, as well as being able to spin stories just the way you want them told, is, in a word, perfect.

A seven-time finalist for the prestigious Romance Writers of America RITA® Award, Maureen is the author of more than one hundred romance novels. Her books regularly appear on the bestseller lists and have won several awards, including the Prism, The National Readers' Choice Award, The Colorado Award of Excellence and the Golden Quill.

One of her books, *The Soul Collector,* was made into a CBS-TV movie starring Melissa Gilbert, Bruce Greenwood and Ossie Davis. If you look closely, in the last five minutes of the movie, you'll spot Maureen, who was an extra in the last scene.

Maureen believes that laughter goes hand in hand with love, so her stories are always filled with humor. The many letters she receives assures her that her readers love to laugh as much as she does.

Maureen Child is a native Californian, but has recently moved to the mountains of Utah. She loves a new adventure, though the thought of having to deal with snow for the first time is a little intimidating.

To Rosemary Rangel Estrada
We really miss you, neighbor!

# One

*Amanda Altman's back in town.*

It was all anyone could talk about and Nathan Battle was getting pretty damn sick of it. Nothing he hated more than being at the center of a gossip tornado. He'd already lived through it once, years ago. Of course, he'd escaped the worst of it by moving to Houston and burying himself in the police academy and then his job.

Wouldn't work this time. He'd built his place here. He wasn't going anywhere. Mostly because Nathan Battle didn't run. So he'd just have to ride this mess out until the town found something new to chew on.

But that was life in Royal, Texas. A town too small to mind its own business and too big to have to repeat the same gossip over and over again.

Even here, he thought, in the hallowed halls of the Texas Cattleman's Club, Nathan couldn't escape the talk—or the speculation. Not even from his best friend.

"So, Nathan," Chance asked with a knowing grin, "you see Amanda yet?"

Nathan looked at the man sitting opposite him. Chance McDaniel owned McDaniel's Acres, a working dude ranch and hotel just south of town. The man had built the place from the ground up on property he'd inherited from his family, and he'd done a hell of a job.

Chance's blond hair was cropped short, but he still couldn't get the wave out of it no matter how he tried. His green eyes were amused and Nathan shook his head, knowing that *he* was the source of his friend's amusement.

"No." One word. Should be concise enough to get his message across. And maybe it would have worked with anyone else. Of course, Nathan told himself wryly, it wouldn't be nearly enough to get Chance to back off. They'd been friends for too long. And nobody knew how to get to you better than a best friend.

"You can't ignore her forever," Chance mused, taking a sip of his scotch.

"It's worked so far," Nathan told him and lifted his own glass for a drink.

"Sure it has," Chance said, muffling a laugh. "That's why you've been such a cool, calm guy the last couple of weeks."

Nathan narrowed his eyes on his friend. "Funny."

"You have no idea," Chance agreed, lips twitching. "So, Sheriff, if you're avoiding the Royal Diner these days, where are you getting your coffee?"

His fingers tightened on the heavy, old crystal. "The gas station."

Now Chance didn't bother to hide his laughter. "You must be desperate if you're drinking the swill Charlie brews down there. You know, maybe it's time you learned how to make decent coffee yourself."

"And maybe it's time you let this go," Nathan told him. Irritating is what it was, he thought. His whole damn routine had been splintered when Amanda moved back home to Royal. Used to be he started off his day with a large coffee and maybe some eggs at the diner. Amanda's sister, Pam, always had his coffee ready for him when he walked in. That was a routine a man could count on. But since Amanda blew back into his world, he'd had to make do with Charlie's disgusting coffee and a packaged sweet roll.

Even when she wasn't trying, Amanda found a way to screw with him.

"Seriously, Nate," Chance said, lowering his voice a little so the other members of the TCC couldn't overhear, "from all reports, Amanda's here to stay. Seems she's been making some changes to the diner, settling in. Even talking about looking for a house of her own, according to Margie Santos."

Nathan had heard all the same talk, of course. Hard not to, when everyone in a ten-mile radius was more than eager to talk to him about Amanda. Margie Rice was the top real estate agent in Royal and one of the biggest gossips as well. If she was spreading the word that Amanda was looking for her own place, then Nathan had to admit that she was here for the long term.

Which meant he couldn't ignore her for much longer.

Too bad, because he'd finally gotten good at not thinking about Amanda. Wasn't always the case. Several years ago, Amanda was *all* Nathan thought about. The passion between them had burned hotter than anything he'd ever known. She'd filled his mind, waking and sleeping.

Of course back then, they'd been engaged.

He scowled into his glass of scotch. *Times change.*

"New subject, Chance," he muttered and let his gaze slide around the main room of the TCC.

While his friend talked about what was happening at the ranch, Nathan's mind wandered. Over the years, it seemed like inside the TCC, time stood still. Even the fact that women were now officially members of the long-standing, males-only club hadn't affected the decor. Paneled walls, dark brown leather furniture—sofas and club chairs—hunting prints on the walls and a big-screen TV so you didn't miss a bit of any Texas sporting event.

The air smelled of lemon polish and the wood floors and tables gleamed in the lamplight. The TV was on now, but muted so that members could sit and brood behind newspapers or chat without having to shout to be heard. The soft clinking of crystal against gleaming wood tables underlined the hushed conversations surrounding them.

A woman's laugh pealed out just then, shattering the quiet and Nathan grinned as he noted that Beau Hacket actually cringed at the sound. At nearly sixty, Beau was short, thick around the middle and with a lot more gray in what was left of his dark red hair. He had a big laugh and a narrow mind—he believed women belonged in the kitchen and didn't care who knew it.

Now, Beau fired a hard look around the room as if to silently say, *Did you all hear that? That's just wrong. Women don't belong here.*

No one said anything, but Nathan read the tension in the room and noted more gritted jaws than usual. Women were members, but they still weren't really welcome. Everyone was gathered for the weekly TCC meeting and none of the old guard were happy about having women included.

"Sounds like Abigail's enjoying herself," Chance muttered into the stillness.

"Abby always enjoys herself," Nathan mused.

Abigail Langley Price, married to Brad Price, had been the first female member of the club. And, of course, she was having a good time now, since she had women to talk to in here. But it hadn't been easy on her, gaining acceptance at the TCC. Even with the support of Nathan, Chance and several of the other members, she'd had to fight her way in—and Nathan admired that about her.

"Does it feel weird to you," Chance asked, "to have women in the club now?"

"Nope." Nathan finished off his scotch and set the empty glass down on the table in front of him. "Felt weirder when they weren't allowed in here."

"Yeah," his friend said. "I know what you mean." Leaning forward, he braced his elbows on his knees. "But men like Beau over there aren't happy about it."

Nathan shrugged. "Men like Beau are always complaining about something. Besides, he and the others are just gonna have to get used to it." Then he added what he'd been thinking a few minutes ago. "Times change."

"They really do," Chance agreed. "Like, for example, the vote we're taking tonight."

Relieved to be off the subject of Amanda, Nathan turned his thoughts to the upcoming vote. It had been the talk of the town for days. Once Abigail and the other women became members of the TCC they'd had some ideas of their own to put forth and tonight marked the vote for one of the biggest items.

"The child-care center?" Nathan asked and Chance nodded.

"It's a big deal and only going to make the hard-line members more irritated than ever."

"True," Nathan agreed, imagining the fireworks that would soon take place over the vote. "Only makes sense if you think about it, though. A safe place for the kids while their parents are here. Probably should have done it years ago."

"Right there with ya," Chance told him with a

shake of his head. "But I'm not sure Beau's going to agree with that."

"Beau doesn't agree with anything," Nathan said with a chuckle. As town sheriff, Nathan had to deal with Beau Hacket on a regular basis. The man had a complaint about everything and everyone, and didn't mind taking up the sheriff's time with them. "A more contrary man has never lived."

"True."

The clock over the river-stone fireplace began to chime the hour and both of them stood up.

"Guess it's time to get the meeting started."

"This should be good," Chance told Nathan and followed him down the hallway to the official meeting room.

An hour later, the arguments were still being shouted out. Beau Hacket had some support for his Neanderthal opinions. Sam and Josh Gordon, the twins who owned and operated Gordon Construction, were getting to be just as hardheaded as Beau.

"Is it just me," Nate whispered to his friend

Alex Santiago, "or is Sam Gordon starting to become more and more like Beau Hacket?"

Alex shifted a look at the twin who was spouting all the reasons why children didn't belong in the TCC.

"It's not just you," he answered quietly. "Even his twin looks surprised at Sam's arguments."

Alex hadn't lived in Royal very long, but he'd made lots of friends in town and seemed to already have a handle on the town and its citizens. A venture capitalist and investor, Alex was wealthy and had become, in his short time in Royal, very influential. Sometimes Nate wondered why a man as rich as Alex would choose to settle down in Royal. But at the same time, he told himself with a smile, people probably wondered why Nathan Battle chose to be the town sheriff. Since he owned half of the Battlelands Ranch, Nate was rich enough to not have to work at all.

But then what the hell would he do?

Shaking his head, Nate gave a quick look around the long table at the members gathered. Not all of them were present, of course, but there were more than enough for the voting. Ryan Grant, former rodeo star, was attending his first official meeting and Nate saw the bemusement in the other man's eyes. Dave Firestone, whose ranch ran alongside Nathan's family spread, was lounging in a chair, watching the goings-on as if he were at a tennis match. Beau was nearly purple in the face, shouting down anyone who argued with him. Chance was sitting beside Shannon Morrison, who looked as if she wanted to stand up and tell Beau Hacket exactly what he could do with his outdated opinions.

And then there was Gil Addison, the TCC president, standing at the head of the table. His dark eyes flashed and Nate knew that his friend had about reached the limits of his patience.

Almost at once, Gil slammed his gavel onto its pedestal until he had quiet. The echoes of arguments and recriminations were hanging in the still air like battle flags when Gil said, "Enough talking. Time for a vote. All in favor of the child-care center being added to the TCC, say 'aye.'"

All of the women, including Missy Reynolds and Vanessa Woodrow, spoke up, but Nathan,

Alex, Chance and several of the others were quick to contribute their votes.

"All opposed," Gil added, "say 'no.'"

A few loud voices were heard.

The gavel slammed down again sharply. Gil nodded at the group and smiled. "Motion's passed. A child-care center will be added to the Texas Cattlemen's Club."

Beau and a few of the other members, still bristling over the fact that women were now included in their group, were practically apoplectic. But, there was nothing they could do about it.

As Beau stormed out of the meeting, Nathan watched him go and almost felt a flicker of sympathy. He could see the other side of the situation, but you couldn't stay locked in the past. The world moved every damn day and you moved with it or you got steamrolled. Tradition was one thing, being stuck in the mud was another.

Change happened whether you liked it or not, so the best way to handle it was to hop on board the train as opposed to stretching your body across the tracks and being run over. Which was, he told himself, a good way to think about how to deal with Amanda.

"This is great," Abigail Price said with a wide smile for her friends and those who had supported them. "And our Julia will be the first child enrolled as soon as we're up and running."

"You bet she will, honey." Brad Price gave his wife's hand a squeeze. "Shame Beau and the rest are upset, but they'll get over it."

"You did," Abigail reminded him with a smile.

True enough, Nate mused thoughtfully. Not too long ago, Brad and Abby were butting heads every chance they got. He'd done his best to keep Abby out of the TCC and now just look at them—in love, married, and with a great little girl.

While everyone around them talked, Alex suggested, "Why don't we head over to the diner and get some coffee and pie?"

"Good idea," Chance agreed and flicked a glance at Nathan.

Friends could be a real pain in the ass sometimes, Nathan told himself. These two were trying to maneuver him into a meeting with Amanda and it just wasn't going to work. He'd see her. In his own time. In his own way. And damned if he was going to put on a show for the folks in Royal.

"No thanks," he said, pushing up from the table. He didn't even look at the other members in the room. "I'm headed back to the office to finish up some paperwork, then I'm going home."

"Still in hiding?" Alex murmured.

Nathan bristled. "Pretty hard to hide in a town the size of Royal."

"You should keep that in mind," Chance told him.

Irritated, Nathan just gritted his teeth and left. *No point in arguing with a jackass,* he thought.

Amanda was so busy she almost didn't have time to worry about Nathan.

Almost.

Turns out, even running the family diner, looking for a new house and arranging to have the transmission in her car replaced *still* left her brain enough room to plague her with thoughts of Nathan Battle.

"Bound to happen," she reassured herself for the fortieth time that morning. Just being in

Royal had brought the memories rushing back and, there were a *lot* of memories.

She'd known Nathan most of her life and had been nuts about him since she was thirteen. She could still remember the sharp, bright thrill of having Nathan, then an all-powerful senior, taking a lowly freshman to the senior prom.

"And, if we'd just stopped it right there, it would be all sunshine and roses," she murmured as she refilled the coffee urn with water, then measured in fresh coffee grounds.

She pushed the button to start the brewing process, then turned to look out at the diner. Even with the changes she'd made in the last couple of weeks, being in this place was as good as being home.

She'd grown up in her parents' diner, working as a busgirl, and then a waitress when she was old enough. The Royal Diner was an institution in town and she was determined that it stay that way. Which was why she'd come home after her father's death to help her older sister, Pam, run the place.

As that reminder rolled through her mind,

Amanda squared her shoulders and nodded briefly to herself. She hadn't come home because of Nathan Battle. Even though a shiver swept through her at just the thought of his name, she discounted it as sense memory. Didn't mean a thing. Her life was different now.

*She* was different now.

"Amanda, my love, when're you going to marry me and run off to Jamaica?"

Startled out of her thoughts, Amanda smiled at the familiar voice and turned to look at Hank Bristow. At eighty, Hank was tall and thin and his skin was craggy from a lifetime spent in the sun. Now that his sons ran the family ranch, Hank spent most of his time in the diner, talking with his friends. His blue eyes twinkled as he held out his cup for a refill.

"Hank, you just love me for my coffee," she told him, pouring a stream of the hot, fresh brew into his cup.

"A woman who can make good coffee?" Hank shook his head and said solemnly, "Worth her weight in gold."

She smiled, patted his hand, then carried the

carafe along the length of the counter, chatting with her customers, freshening coffee as she went. It was all so familiar. So…easy. She'd slid into life in Royal as smoothly as if she'd never left.

"Why did you order new menus?"

Okay, not completely smoothly. Amanda turned to face Pam. As usual, the shorter woman didn't look happy with her. But then, the two of them had never been close. Not growing up. Not now. Even though Amanda had primarily come back to Royal because Pam had needed help running the diner. But, she supposed, *needing* help and *wanting* it were two different things.

Amanda walked the length of the counter again, and set the coffeepot down on the warmer before she answered.

"Because the old ones needed to be replaced," she said. "The laminate was cracked and old and the menus themselves were outdated." Catching the look of interest on Hank's face, Amanda lowered her voice. "We don't even serve half the things listed anymore, Pam."

Her sister's chin-length brown hair was tucked

behind her ears. She wore a red T-shirt and jeans and a pair of scarlet sandals wrapped around her feet. She was tapping the toe of one sandal against the shining linoleum floor. "But our regular customers know that. They don't need fancy new menus, Amanda."

She sighed, but stood her ground. "They're not fancy, Pam. They're just not ratty."

Pam hissed in a breath.

"Okay, sorry." Amanda dug deep for patience and said, "We're in this together, right? You said you needed help and I came home. The Altman sisters running the diner. Together."

Pam thought about that for a long second before finally shrugging. "As long as you remember I didn't ask you to come in and take over."

"I'm not taking over, Pam. I'm trying to help."

"By changing everything?" Pam's voice spiked, then she seemed to realize that everyone in the place was no doubt listening because she spoke more softly when she continued. "There's such a thing as tradition around here, you know. Or did you forget, living off in Dallas for so long?"

A small twinge of guilt nibbled at her insides.

Amanda hadn't been around much the last few years, it was true. And she should have been. She knew that, too. It had been just Amanda, Pam and their father, since her mother had died years before and the three of them had sort of drifted apart. For the rest of her life, she knew she'd regret not spending more time with her dad when she had the chance.

But she had grown up in the diner just as Pam had. Changing things wasn't easy for her, either. A part of her hated getting rid of things that her father had put in place. But times changed whether you wanted them to or not.

"Dad told us himself that when he took over the diner from *his* father, he made lots of changes," she argued, defending the new, still red—but unscarred red—counter and tables.

Pam scowled at her. "That's not the point."

Amanda took a deep breath and inhaled the aroma of fresh coffee, eggs and bacon. "Then what is the point, Pam? You asked me to come home and help, remember?"

"Help, not take over."

Okay, maybe she had been a little quick with

changes. Maybe she hadn't taken the time to include her sister in decisions being made. That was her fault and she was willing to take the blame for it. In her defense, Pam had made herself scarce since Amanda got back to town. But, if she mentioned that, it would only start a new argument, so she let it go.

"You're right," Amanda said and watched surprise flicker in her sister's eyes. "I should have talked to you about the menus. About the countertops and tables and I didn't. I just..." She paused to look around the diner before adding, "I guess I didn't realize how much I'd missed this place. And when I got home, I just dove right in."

"I can't believe you missed the diner," Pam muttered.

Amanda laughed. "I know. Me, neither. You and I spent so much time working here as kids, who knew that I'd look forward to working here again?"

Pam sighed and leaned against the counter. She shot a frown at Hank, who was still listening in. The old man rolled his eyes and looked away.

"It's good you're here," Pam finally said. "And

between the two of us, we should be able to both run the diner *and* have lives."

"We will," Amanda said, smiling a little at the tiny bridge suddenly springing up between the sisters.

"But it *is* the two of us, Amanda," Pam told her firmly. "You don't get to make all the decisions and then let me find out later when the new menus arrive."

"Absolutely," she said. "You're right. I should have talked to you and I will from now on."

"Good." Pam nodded. "That's good. Now, I'm heading out. I've got a line on a new supplier of organic vegetables and—"

Amanda smiled and let her mind wander while her sister rattled off information on local farmers. Her gaze slid across the familiar faces filling the diner, then drifted out to the street beyond the wide glass windows. Main Street in Royal. Sidewalks crowded with early shoppers. Cars parked haphazardly along the curb. The sheriff stepping off the sidewalk, headed for the diner.

*Sheriff. Headed for the diner.*

Amanda's heart jumped in her chest. Her mouth

went dry and her gaze locked on the one man in the world she couldn't seem to forget.

Nathan knew it was past time to face Amanda. He left the sheriff's office with his deputy, Red Hawkins, in charge and stepped out onto Main Street. The morning was clear and promised another red-hot day. Summer in Texas was already off to a blistering start. The sun was a ball of fire looking to combust.

God, he loved it.

Walking down the sidewalk, his boots clattering out a sharp rhythm, Nathan nodded at those he passed and paused to hold a door for Macy Harris as she struggled to carry a baby and cling to her toddler's hand.

This was his place. Where he belonged. He'd actually had to leave and spend a few years in Houston as a city cop to figure that out. But now that he was back, Nathan knew he'd never leave Royal again. He'd found his place and damned if he was going to let Amanda Altman make him uncomfortable in it.

He loped across the street, dodging the occasional car, and headed straight for the Royal Diner.

The place was a landmark in town. He could remember going there as a kid with his folks and then later, as a teenager, he'd gathered there with his friends after football games and on long, boring summer afternoons.

It was the unofficial heart of town, which meant that at any time during the day, there would be a crowd inside. A crowd that would watch his and Amanda's first meeting with interest.

"Well, hell," he muttered as he marched up to the glass door. "Might as well get it done and let the gossips loose."

He pulled the door open, stepped inside and stopped, letting his gaze slide over the familiar surroundings. *Mostly* familiar, he corrected silently.

The walls had been painted. No longer a bright white that seemed to sear your eyes on a hot summer day, the walls were now a soft green, dotted with framed photos of Royal through the years. The counter had been changed, too—the old chipped and scarred red was now a shining sweep of a deeper, richer red. The black-and-white checked floors had been polished and the red vinyl booth seats had all been revamped. There were new chairs pulled up to the scatter of tables and sunshine streamed through the windows lining Main Street.

But none of it really mattered to him.

How could it?

He was too focused on the woman standing behind that new counter, staring at him.

Amanda Altman.

*Damn.* She looked way too good.

Nathan took a breath, forcing air into lungs suddenly starving for sustenance. He hadn't really expected to feel the rush of heat swamping him. He'd convinced himself he was over her. Had forgotten what it had been like to be with her.

Big mistake.

"Hello, Nathan."

"Amanda," he said and ignored the swell of whispers sliding around the room as if carried along by a west Texas wind.

She moved toward the end of the counter, positioning herself behind the cash register. Defensive move?

Oddly enough, that eased him some. Knowing she was no happier about this public meeting than he was took some of the pressure off. In fact, he thought, it sort of tossed the power back into his lap.

She was new here. Okay, yeah, she'd grown up in Royal, just as he had. But Nathan had been here for the last three years and she'd been back in town only a couple of weeks. He'd made his place here and she was still treading water.

With that thought firmly in mind, he walked toward her and noted her chin came up defiantly. Damned if he hadn't missed that stubborn move of hers.

"Morning, Nathan," Pam chirped loudly. "We've missed you in here lately."

"Been busy," he said and ignored Hank Bristow's snort of derision.

"You want your usual?"

"That'd be good, Pam, thanks," he said, his gaze never leaving Amanda's.

She looked the same and yet...different. Maybe

it was just that she was older now. Maybe it was the fact that her eyes weren't shining with adoration when she looked up at him. Didn't matter, he assured himself. Amanda was his past, in spite of his body's reaction to her.

"So," he said, knowing everyone in the diner was holding their breath, waiting to hear what might happen next, "you back to stay or this just a visit?"

Pam walked up to him then and handed him a to-go cup filled with black coffee. He didn't even glance at her as he took it and reached into his pocket for cash.

"On the house," Amanda told him.

"Not necessary," Nathan said and laid a couple of dollars on the counter. "You didn't answer the question, Amanda. You here to stay or just blowin' through?"

"I'm home to stay, Nathan," Amanda said. "I hope that won't be a problem for you."

He laughed shortly, and took a sip of coffee. Deliberately then, he said loudly enough for everyone to hear, "Why would that be a problem for me, Amanda? You and I are long since done."

He could almost *see* every customer in the place perking up their ears and leaning in closer so as not to miss a single word.

"You're right," Amanda said, lifting her chin even higher. "We're not kids anymore. There's no reason why we can't be friendly."

Friendly? His entire body was jittering with heat and she thought they could be friends? Not a chance. But he wasn't going to give her the satisfaction of knowing that.

"None at all," Nathan agreed tightly.

"Good. I'm glad that's settled," she said.

"Me, too."

"Oh, yeah," Hank muttered with a snort. "We can all see that this has worked out fine."

"Butt out, Hank," Nathan told him and turned for the door.

"Walk me to my car, Nathan?" Pam blurted and had him stopping for one last look behind him. But instead of seeing the woman headed toward him, his gaze darted straight to Amanda and he felt a surge of heat zap him.

The past might be dead and gone, but whatever

hummed between them had just enough life left in it to be annoying.

When Pam threaded her arm through his, Nathan led her out and didn't bother looking back again.

# Two

"That went well," Amanda told herself as she entered the tiny apartment over the diner that was now home.

All day, she'd been thinking about that brief, all-too-public meeting with Nathan. Which was, she thought grimly, probably exactly what he'd been hoping for. Nathan had always been the kind of man to assume command of any given situation. He was the take-charge type and so it was like him to make sure their first meeting was just the way *he* wanted it. That's why he'd come into the diner during the morning bustle—so that there would be so many witnesses to their conversation, neither one of them could really *talk.*

Honestly, the man hadn't changed a bit. Still stiff-necked and hardheaded. She'd seen that familiar, stony glint in his eye that morning and known the minute he opened his mouth that nothing between them would be settled. But then, she thought, why would it be?

She dropped onto an overstuffed, floral sofa that was older than she was, and propped her feet on the narrow coffee table in front of her. The romance novel she was currently reading lay beside an old ceramic pitcher filled with daisies and bluebells. Their scent was a soft sigh of summer in the too-warm room and, not for the first time, Amanda wished the apartment boasted more than a thirty-year-old air conditioner with a habit of shutting down every now and then for no particular reason.

The sofa held bright, boldly colored accent pillows and the two chairs in the room were more comfortable to look at than they were for sitting. There were pictures on the walls, a few throw rugs across the scarred wooden floor and the walls were still the dusty sand color Amanda's mother had preferred.

Folding her arms over her chest, Amanda stared up at the lazily spinning ceiling fan. A tired breeze of air sulkily drifted over her. This little apartment above the diner was like a security blanket. Her parents had lived here when they first married and opened the diner. Then later, they'd rented it out, furnished, to different people over the years. Pam had lived here for a while, then it had been Amanda's turn while she was in college. Having her own place had given her the chance to find her independence while staying close enough to home to feel safe.

Plus, she and Nathan had met here a lot back in those days. Those memories were imprinted on the tiny apartment, with its outdated, yet cozy furniture. If she tried, Amanda thought she'd be able to hear his voice, whispering to her in the dark.

She didn't try.

Instead, she concentrated on what he'd had to say that morning. Or rather what he *hadn't* said.

"He didn't want to talk anything through," she

said to the empty room and paused, as if waiting for the shadows to agree with her. "He only wanted to let me know that seeing me again meant nothing. He was trying to lay down the rules. Just like before. He tells you what things will be like, lays out his orders, then steps back, giving you room to follow them."

Well, he was in for a shock. She didn't *take* orders anymore. In fact, looking back at the girl she had once been made her nearly cringe. Back then, she'd been young enough and in love enough, that she had never once argued with Nathan—at least until that last night. When he announced his choice of a movie, she hadn't said she hated action movies. She'd never told him that she didn't like going to car shows or that she found fishing to be the most boring activity in the world.

Nope. Instead, Amanda had sat through countless movies where the only storyline revolved around demolition. She'd spent interminably long days watching Nathan fish in local streams and rivers and she didn't want to think about the hours lost staring at car engines.

Looking back now, Amanda couldn't believe

how completely she'd given herself up to Nathan. Then, he was all she had cared about. All she thought about. And when everything fell apart between them…she'd had no idea what to do with herself.

It had taken a while to find her feet. To find *Amanda.* But she'd done it and there was no going back now—even if she wanted to, which she *so* did not.

Lifting her chin, she narrowed her eyes on the fan blades as if facing down Nathan himself. "I'm all grown up now, Nathan. I'm not going to roll over and speak on command. I don't *need* you anymore."

As her own words rang out in the room, Amanda gave a tight smile. Good words. Now if she could just *believe* them.

Oh, she didn't need Nathan like she had then. Like she had needed air. Water. No, now what she needed was to get rid of the memories. To clear Nathan Battle out of her mind and heart once and for all, so she could move on. So she could stop remembering that when things were good between them, they were *very* good.

What she had to concentrate on, she told herself firmly as she leaped off the couch to pace the confines of the small living area, was the bad parts. The times Nathan had made her crazy. The dictatorial Nathan who had tried to make every decision for her. The man who had insisted they marry because she was pregnant, then the minute that pregnancy was over, had walked away from her so fast, she'd seen nothing but a blur.

*That* was what she had to remember. The pain of not only losing the baby she'd had such dreams for, but also realizing that the man she loved wasn't the man she'd thought he was.

If she could just do that, she'd be fine.

She walked to the galley-style kitchen and rummaged in the fridge for some of yesterday's leftovers. Working with food all day pretty much ensured that she wasn't hungry enough to cook for herself in the evening. But tonight, pickings were slim. A bowl of the diner's five-star chili, a few sandwiches and a plate of double-stuffed baked potatoes that hadn't sold the day before.

None of it looked tempting, but she knew she had to eat. So she grabbed the potatoes—and a bottle of chardonnay—then closed the fridge. She pulled out a cookie sheet, lined the potatoes up on it and put it in the oven. Once the temperature was set, she poured herself a glass of wine and carried it with her to the doll-sized bathroom.

It only took her a few minutes to shower and change into a pair of cutoff jean shorts and a tank top. Then she took her wine and walked barefoot back to the living room to wait for dinner.

The crisp, cold wine made the waiting easier to take. Heck, it even made thoughts of Nathan less...disturbing. What did it say about her, she wondered, that even when she was furious with the man, she still felt that buzz of something amazing?

Sad, sad Amanda.

In the years since she and Nathan had broken up, she hadn't exactly lived like a nun. She'd had dates. Just not many. But how could she think about a future when the past kept rising up in her mind? It always came back to Nathan. When she met a man, she waited, hoping to feel that special *zing* she had only found with Nathan. And it was never there.

How could she possibly agree to marry someone else if Nathan was the one who made her body burn? Was she supposed to settle? Impossible. She wanted what she'd once had. She just wanted it with someone else.

Heck, she had known Nathan was there the minute he'd walked into the diner. She hadn't had to see him. She'd *felt* his presence—like the electricity in the air just before a thunderstorm. And that first look into his eyes had jolted her so badly, it had been all she could do to lock her knees into place so she wouldn't melt into an embarrassing puddle of goo.

No one else had ever done that to her.

Only him.

She took a sip of her wine and shook her head. "This is not a good sign, Amanda."

It had been *years* since she'd seen him, touched him, and it might as well have been yesterday from the way her own body was reacting. Every cell inside her was jumping up and down, rolling out the red carpet and putting on a party hat.

But there weren't going to be any parties. Not

with Nathan, at any rate. She'd never get him out of her system if she let him back in.

Trying to distract herself from the hormonal rodeo going on inside her, she walked to one of the windows overlooking Main Street and looked out at Royal. Only a few cars on the road and almost no pedestrians. The silence was staggering. Streetlights dropped puddles of yellow light on the empty sidewalks and, above the town, a clear night sky displayed thousands of stars.

Life in a small town was vastly different than what she'd known the last few years living in Dallas. There, the city bustled with life all night. Shops and clubs and bars glittered with neon lights so bright, they blotted out the stars overhead. Tourists flocked to the city to spend their money, and the nightlife was as busy as the daytime crowds.

It had been so different from the way she'd grown up, such a distraction from the pain she was in—Amanda had really enjoyed city life. At first. But over time, she had become just another nameless person rushing through the crowds, going from work to an apartment and back again the next day. Nights were crowded with noise and people and the gradual realization that she wasn't happy.

Her life had become centered around a job she didn't really like and a nightlife she didn't actually enjoy. She had a few friends and a few dates that always seemed to end badly—probably her own fault since she never had been able to meet a man without comparing him to Nathan. Pitiful, really, but there it was.

Then her father passed away and, a few months later, she got the call for help from Pam. Even knowing that she would have to eventually deal with Nathan again, Amanda had left the big city behind and rushed back home to Royal.

And she had slid back into life here as easily as if she'd never left. The truth was, she was really a small-town girl at heart.

She liked a town where nighttime brought quiet and families gathered together. She liked knowing that she was safe—without having to have two or three locks on her apartment door. And, right now, she liked knowing that she wouldn't have to talk to anyone until at least tomorrow morning.

She could have stayed at her family home, where Pam was living. But Amanda had become accustomed to having her own space. Besides, as evidenced by her sister's behavior today, just because Pam had needed her help didn't mean that she wanted Amanda around. She'd never been close with her sister and, so far, that situation looked as though it wasn't going to change any.

She took another sip of her wine and let that thought, along with all the thoughts of Nathan, slide from her mind. She wasn't going to solve everything in one night, so why drive herself nuts?

Her gaze slid to the darkened sheriff's office. No one was there, of course. In a town the size of Royal, you didn't need an on-duty police presence twenty-four hours a day. Besides, Nathan and his deputy were only a phone call away.

She wondered if Nathan still lived out on his family's ranch, the Battlelands. Then she reminded herself firmly it was none of her business where Nathan lived.

"Thinking about him is *not* the way to stop thinking about him," she told herself aloud.

The scent of melting cheese and roasting potatoes was beginning to fill the air and her stomach rumbled. Apparently she was hungrier than she had thought.

When the knock sounded on her door, she was more surprised than anything else. She took a step forward, then stopped, staring at the door leading to the outside staircase at the side of the diner. A ripple of something familiar sneaked across her skin and she took a gulp of her wine to ease the sensation. Didn't really help. But then, nothing could. Because she *knew* who was knocking on her door.

When she was steady enough, she walked to the door and asked unnecessarily, "Who is it?"

"It's me, Amanda." It was Nathan's voice, low and commanding. "Open up."

Wow. Skitters of expectation jolted through her. Amazing that just his voice could do that to her. After all these years, he could still stir her up without even trying.

She put one hand flat against the door and

she could have sworn that she actually felt heat sliding through the wood. She took a breath, smoothed out her voice and tried to do the same for her racing heart. It didn't work.

"What do you want, Nathan?" she asked, leaning her forehead against the door panel.

"What I want is to not be standing out here talking through a door where anyone in Royal can see me."

Not that there were a lot of people out there at night. But all it would take was one busybody happening to glance up and word would fly all over town. *Nathan was at Amanda's doorstep last night!*

*Okay,* she thought, straightening, *good motivation for opening the door.* So she did.

Under the porch light, his brown hair looked lighter, his shoulders looked broader and his eyes…too shadowed to read. But then, she thought, it wasn't difficult to guess what he was thinking, feeling. His stance was stiff, his jaw tight. He looked as though he'd rather be anywhere but there.

Well, fine. She hadn't invited him, had she? "What is it, Nathan?"

He scowled at her and stepped inside.

"Please," she said, sarcasm dripping as she closed the door against the hot, humid air, "come in."

"We have to talk," he said, striding across the room before turning to face her. "And damned if I'm going to do it in the diner with everyone in town listening in."

Her fingers tightened on her wineglass. "Then maybe you shouldn't have come into the diner this morning."

"Maybe," he muttered and stuffed both hands into the pockets of his jeans. "But I needed some decent coffee."

She hadn't expected that. But he looked so disgusted, so…frustrated, Amanda laughed. His head snapped up, his gaze boring into hers.

"I'm sorry," she said, shaking her head as another laugh bubbled out. "But really? Coffee is what finally brought you in?"

"I've been getting mine at the gas station."

"Poor guy," she said, and he frowned at the humor in her voice.

"You can laugh. But I don't think Charlie's so much as rinsed out that coffeepot of his in twenty years." He grimaced at the thought and made Amanda smile again.

Shaking his head, he nodded at the wine in her hand. "You have any more of that?"

"I do. Also have beer, if you'd rather."

"Yeah, that'd be good." Some of the tension left his shoulders and one corner of his mouth tilted up into what might have been a half smile if it hadn't disappeared so fast.

She walked to the kitchen, opened the fridge and pulled out a beer. Amanda paused for a second to get her bearings. The moment she'd been dreading for years was finally here. Nathan and her were together again. Alone. And there was just no telling what might happen next. But whatever it was, she thought, at least it would be *something.* Better than the vacuum they'd been in for the last few years. Better than the rigid silence that had stretched between them since she came back to Royal.

With that thought in mind, she walked to the living room, handed him the cold bottle, then took a seat on the couch. Mainly because her knees felt a little wobbly.

Looking up at him, she watched as he opened the beer and took a drink. He looked so good it was irritating. His skin was tanned and there was a slightly paler line across the top of his forehead where his hat usually rested. His brown eyes were watchful as he glanced around the apartment, no doubt taking in everything in that all-encompassing sweep. She wondered if he was remembering all the nights they'd been together, here in this room. Could he still hear the whispered words between them? Probably not, she thought. Nathan wouldn't want to be reminded of a past that had no bearing on his life anymore.

She studied him as he studied the apartment. He wore scuffed brown boots, blue jeans and a short-sleeved, dark green T-shirt with Battlelands Ranch emblazoned on the shirt pocket. He stood stiff and straight as if awaiting a military inspection.

He was off-duty and yet everything about

him screamed *police.* Nathan was just that kind of man. Devoted to duty, he preferred order to chaos, rules to confusion. He would take a road trip and stay on the highway, where Amanda would prefer the back roads, stopping at everything interesting along the way. No wonder they had clashed.

And even knowing all of that, she still felt the rush of attraction that she couldn't deny. She *wanted* to be immune to him and, clearly, she wasn't.

But this was exactly why she needed to be here. Because until she *was* immune to Nathan Battle, she'd never be able to move on. Instead, she'd go on being haunted by memories, by thoughts of what might have been.

He took another drink of his beer and looked down at the bottle in his hand. "I was sorry about your dad."

She blinked against the sudden sting of tears. The one thing she hadn't expected from Nathan was kindness. It was…disarming. "Thanks. I miss him."

"Yeah, he was a good man."

"He was." Safe ground. Talk about their families. Don't mention the tension coiled so tightly between them.

"Why did you come back?"

And *there* was the Nathan she knew best. So much for the pleasantries—it was on to Round One. "Excuse me?"

"Well, hell, Amanda." He frowned down at her and looked a little surprised that she didn't seem affected by his displeasure. "You were gone for years. Why come back at all?"

"Are you in charge of Royal's borders now, *Sheriff?*" she asked. "Do people have to check in with you before they move in?"

"I didn't say that."

She pushed to her feet. Even though she stood five foot ten, she was forced to tip her head back to meet his gaze, but she did it. "Royal's my home as much as it is yours, Nathan Battle."

"Couldn't tell from how you acted," he said, completely ignoring the hard glare she fired at him.

"I seem to recall you living in Houston for quite

a while. Were you interrogated when you moved back home?"

"I'm not interrogating you, Amanda," he countered. "I'm just asking a damn question."

"That you already know the answer to," she shot back. "Pam needed help with the diner. I came home. That's the story. None of this concerns you, Nathan. This is my business."

"Damn straight it is, but now that you're back, it's *my* business, too." He stood as still and cold as a statue.

"How do you figure?"

"I'm the sheriff here. This is where I live. For you to come back now and start stirring things—"

"What am I stirring, Nathan?" she interrupted, and saw with a jolt of glee that he still hated being cut off. It infuriated her to remember that in the old days. She'd have shut her mouth so he could keep talking. Well, that time was gone. "I'm working at my family's diner."

"And getting tongues wagging again," he pointed out.

"Please. People in Royal gossip about everything. I didn't have to *be* here to have them talk about me."

"They're not talking about you," he elaborated grimly. "They're talking about *us.*"

"There is no us," she said flatly, and was surprised by the twinge of pain that clutched at her heart.

"I know that and you know that, but the folks in town—"

"Forget about them," she interrupted again.

He took a long deep breath from between clenched teeth. "Easy for you to say. But as sheriff, I need to have the respect of the people I'm protecting. I don't like being the subject of gossip."

"Then tell them that. Why tell me?"

"Because if you leave, it'll stop."

She set her wineglass down before she was tempted to throw it at his rock-hard head. "I'm not leaving. And, it'll never stop, Nathan."

That statement hit him hard. She saw the proof of it flicker in his eyes. But she wasn't finished.

"Until we're ninety, people around here will be speculating and remembering…."

"Damn it, Amanda, I want you out of town."

"And I want you to stop caring what other people think," she snapped. "I guess we're both doomed to disappointment."

He set his beer bottle on the table beside her glass and moved in on her. He was so tall, he didn't have to put much effort into looming. She supposed it just came naturally to a man used to having his own way. A man accustomed to telling people what to do and having them do it.

It might have worked on her years ago, Amanda told herself, but no more. She was her own woman now. She made her own choices and decisions and lived with the consequences. She wouldn't be ordered out of town and she wouldn't be scared off by a big, gorgeous sheriff with eyes as cold as a winter wind.

"If you think you're worrying me, you're wrong."

"I don't want you worried."

"Good, because—"

"I don't want you at all."

Direct hit, she thought, as an icy fist slammed into her chest and squeezed her heart. But she wouldn't let him see it. "I don't want you, either, Nathan. I'm not that young girl anymore, dazzled because Nathan Battle noticed her. I'm not going to follow you around all doe-eyed, hoping for a smile from you. I'm—"

He grabbed her, yanked her close and kissed her with a fierce desperation that was fueled by desire and anger, all twisted up together. She could feel it in him as she felt it in herself. Past and present tangled together and memories were as thick as honey on a winter morning.

But those memories were swamped by all of the new sensations coursing through her. Amanda didn't try to pull free. Didn't pretend that she wasn't as hungry for him as he was for her. Instead, she moved into him, wrapped her arms around his neck and held on.

*This* is what she'd missed for so long. This man's touch. His kiss. The feel of his hard, strong body pushed up close against hers. She parted her lips for him and took him inside her. When he groaned and held her even tighter, Amanda felt bolts of heat shoot through her system like a summer lightning storm. So much electricity between them. So much heat.

Was it any wonder they had flashed and burned out too quickly?

His hands slid up and down her back, holding her, pressing her as close as he could. His mouth took hers again and again, and she met every stroke of his tongue with eager abandon. God, she'd missed him. Missed *them.* She had found nothing that could compare to what happened when they came together. No other man she'd ever met could compare to Nathan. Which meant that she was in very deep trouble.

Her mind raced even as her body lit up like a sparkler factory. This was a huge mistake. Falling into Nathan's arms was *not* the way to get over him. But right now, all she was interested in was feeling her body come back to life as if waking up after a seven-year nap. Her skin tingled, her heartbeat crashing in her chest, and in the pit of her belly, heat settled and began to spread.

What was wrong with her, anyway?

# Three

When Nathan suddenly released her and took one long step back and away, Amanda swayed unsteadily and gasped for air like a drowning woman. Her mouth burned from his kiss and her body was trembling.

"See?" he practically growled at her. "*This* is why you shouldn't have come back home."

"What?" She blinked up at him and saw that, once again, Nathan's expression seemed to be etched into stone. He looked hard, untouchable and about as passionate as a slab of granite. How did he turn it on and off like that? And could he teach her how to do it?

"I kissed you and you were all over me."

A sudden spurt of ice water flowed through her veins and put out all the lingering fires inside. Maybe he wouldn't have to teach her after all.

"Excuse me? I was all over you?" She took a step closer and stabbed her index finger at him. "Just who grabbed who, here? Who came to whose house? Who started kissing?"

His mouth worked and his lips thinned into a tight line. "Not the point."

"It's exactly the point, Nathan." Furious now, more at herself for falling so easily into old habits than at him, Amanda said, "Just like before, *you* came after *me.* You started all of this, then and now."

"And I'm going to end it."

Hurt raged inside, but was soon swallowed by a wave of fury. He decided when to start things. When to end things. And she was supposed to go quietly along. Nathan Battle, Master of the Universe.

"Big surprise. You like ending things, don't you?"

His eyes narrowed on her and his jaw muscle

twitched so violently she was pretty sure he was grinding his teeth into powder. *Well, good.* She'd hate to think she was the only furious one in the room.

"I'm not the one who ended it seven years ago," he finally said, his voice a low throb of barely leashed anger.

"Not how I remember it," Amanda countered, the sting of that long-ago night still as fresh as if it had happened just yesterday. "You're the one who walked out."

"It's what you wanted." His gaze drilled into hers.

She met him glare for glare. "How would you know, Nathan? You never *asked* me what I wanted."

"This is pointless."

A long minute or two of tense silence stretched out between them. The only sound—the oven timer going off—rang out like a bell at a boxing match signaling the end of a round.

It worked to jolt both of them out of their defensive stances and a second later, Nathan was heading for her door. When he got there, he paused and turned back to look at her.

"This town chews on gossip every day, but I'm not going to be gnawed on."

"Good for you!" She picked up her wine and took a swallow she didn't really want before setting the glass down again. If he thought she was looking forward to being the topic of whispered conversations, he was nuts.

"The Battle family has a reputation in this town—"

"And the Altmans aren't in your circle, are we?" she interrupted again and felt a small swift tug of pleasure, knowing it irritated him.

"I didn't say that."

"You didn't have to." Walking toward him, Amanda glared up into his dark brown eyes. "I'm amazed you ever deigned to propose to me in the first place."

If possible, she thought his eyes actually went black for a second or two. How twisted was she that she *still* thought him the most gorgeous man on the planet?

"You were carrying my child," he told her flatly.

That statement, said with such frigid control, sliced at her like a blade and Amanda fought against the pain.

They hadn't spoken about their lost baby since the night he'd walked out on her. For him to bring it up now… "That was low."

He paused for a long minute or so, just studying her through narrowed eyes. "Yeah, it was." He scrubbed one hand across his face. "Damn it, Amanda, we've got to find a way to live in this town together."

She slid her hands up and down her arms. Funny—even with the hot, humid air of summer, she felt a chill. Maybe it was him being here, so close. Maybe it had been the loss of heat when their kiss ended. And maybe, she thought, it was because of the memories he'd brought up and waved in her face.

The memory of the child she'd carried and lost. The baby she had wanted so badly. Whatever it was, she wanted to be alone until that icy sensation was gone. She needed time to herself. To think. To regroup. And she couldn't do that until she convinced Nathan to leave.

"I'm guessing you have a plan," she said with a sigh.

"Damn straight, I do," he told her. "We go about our business. We live our lives. If we see each other, it's friendly, but distant. No more private chats. No—"

"Kissing?" she finished for him.

"Yeah. No more of that."

"Fine. Agreed." She threw both hands high. "Nathan's rules of behavior. Will you print me out a copy? I'll sign it. You want it notarized, too?"

"Funny."

"Well, blast it, Nathan, you haven't changed a bit. Still issuing orders and expecting them to be followed. Who made you the grand pooh-bah of the Western world?"

"Pooh-bah?"

She ignored that. "You come to my house. You kiss me. Then you lay down rules for me to live my life by and what? You expected me to just salute and say, 'Yes, sir'?"

"Would've been nice," he muttered.

She laughed. In spite of everything. "Yeah, well, not going to happen."

"You make me crazy," he admitted, shaking his head slowly. "You always did."

His voice was softer, deeper, and his eyes held a heat she remembered too well. So she stiffened her spine, refusing to be swayed by the urges she felt deep within her.

"Good to know," Amanda said, tipping her head back to look into his eyes. "That's some consolation, anyway."

He blew out a breath and muttered something she didn't quite catch before saying, "Fine. No rules. We go along. Stay out of each other's way."

"Fine."

"Eventually, people will stop talking or waiting for something to happen between us and—"

"You're still doing it," Amanda interrupted.

"Doing what?"

"Making rules. Setting down how things will be," she said. Tipping her head to one side, she stared up at him in complete frustration. "You can't regulate life, Nathan. It just…happens."

Like losing a baby you had loved from the moment of conception. That familiar twinge of pain, muted slightly because of time and her deliberate attempts to bury it, twisted inside her briefly.

"Unacceptable."

"You don't get to make that call, Nathan," she said softly.

"You're wrong." His eyes were hard, flinty chips of frozen chocolate. Whatever softness had been there before had completely dissipated. "My life moves just as I want it to. No exceptions." He paused. "Not anymore."

There it was, she thought. Once upon a time, *she* had been the exception to Nathan's carefully laid-out life. She'd thrown a wrench into his plans, made him scramble for a new strategy and then it had all fallen apart again. This time, though, she was older—and wiser, she hoped—and she wouldn't be sucked into Nathan's tidily arranged world. She preferred her life messy. She liked the adventure of not really knowing what to expect.

Of course, then scenes like tonight would probably rise up again to torture her, but that was a risk she'd rather take. Better than having your life plotted out on a ledger sheet, with no surprises, no jolts of pleasure or pain.

"Royal's a small town," he was saying and Amanda pushed her thoughts aside to pay attention. "But not so small that we can't comfortably ignore each other."

"That's how you want this to play out?" she asked. "We each pretend the other doesn't exist?"

"Better that way," he said.

"For who?"

He didn't answer. He just opened the door and said, "Goodbye, Amanda."

The sound of his boots on the stairs rang out like a too-fast heartbeat. A few seconds later, she heard a car engine fire up and then he was driving away.

Amanda closed her door on the world, wandered to the kitchen and retrieved the stuffed potatoes that were just a little too well-done. She idly stood there and watched steam lift off her dinner and twist in the barely moving air.

"Damn it," she whispered and stared through the window to the night beyond the glass. Her dinner was burned, her stomach was spinning and her temper was at war with her hormones.

Nathan was a force of nature. One that apparently was destined to crash in and out of her life whether she wanted him to or not. And the worst part?

"He walked away. Again."

She poured a fresh glass of wine, forced herself to eat the overdone potatoes and promised herself the next time she and Nathan were in the same room, *she* would be the one doing the walking.

The Battlelands Ranch glowed in the darkness. It stood like a proud dowager, waiting to welcome home its prodigal children. Practically every window shone with lamplight. Even the outbuildings—the barn, the foreman's house and Nathan's own place—boasted porch lights that formed brightly lit pathways.

Just like always, Nathan felt tension slide away as he drove down the oak-lined drive and steered his 4Runner toward the house he'd had built for himself when he moved back to Royal. He might not be a rancher these days, but the land was in his blood as much as it was in his younger brother Jacob's. The Battles had been on this land for more than a hundred and fifty years. They'd carved out every acre. Bled for it. Wept for it, and managed to hold on to it through all the bad times that had come their way.

The heart of the main ranch house was the original structure, a stately Victorian that the first Battle in Texas had built more than a hundred and fifty years ago to please his new bride. Over the years, that turreted, gingerbread-adorned structure had been added to, with wings spreading from each side and spilling into the back. Most of the ranch houses in the area were more modern, of course. Some mansions, some simple houses, they were all interchangeable in Nathan's eyes.

This place was unique because the Battles didn't tear something down just because it was old. They fixed it, improved on it and kept it, always to remind them of where they'd come from. Now that stately old Victorian was the centerpiece of a ranch bigger and more prosperous than that first Battle could ever have dreamed.

Gnarled, twisted live oaks stood like ancient

soldiers on either side of the drive and gathered in clumps along the front and rear of the house. As Nathan parked his car and climbed out, he heard the swish of leaves in the grudgingly moving hot air.

From the main house came the sharp, clear sound of children's laughter, and Nathan smiled to himself. Lots of changes here at the Battlelands—mostly thanks to Jacob and his wife, Terri. They and their three kids were making this place come alive again as it hadn't since Nathan and Jake were kids themselves.

He glanced quickly at the wading pool and the nearby wooden swing set and climbing gym he'd helped Jacob put together for the kids. That laughter spilled from the house again and Nathan instinctively quelled the small twist of envy he felt for what his brother had. He knew Jake was happy. He had a family and the ranch he loved and Nathan didn't begrudge him any of it.

Still, it was a stunner that his younger brother had a wife and kids, but Jake had taken to life as a family man as easily as he had assumed control of the ranch years ago.

Nathan loved the place and it would always be *home* to him, but the ranch had never been at the heart of him as it had for Jake. As long as Nathan could remember, he had wanted to be a cop, while Jake wanted nothing more than to ride the range, and deal with the cattle grazing on the thousands of acres the family claimed. It had worked out well, Nathan told himself. Didn't matter that he was the eldest. It was enough for Nathan that the Battlelands was in good hands—even if those hands weren't *his*.

And, since Terri was pregnant again, Nathan knew that the family ranch was going to be in Battle hands for many more years to come. He couldn't help wondering what Jake thought of that, if his brother ever sat down and realized that his sons and daughters would be working the same land that had been handed down to him.

That twist of envy grabbed at him again and Nathan couldn't help wondering how his life might be right now if Amanda had carried their child to term. Would they still be together? Would there be more children? He tried to imagine it, but couldn't quite pull it off.

The ranch house door opened just then and a spill of light from inside poured onto the wide front porch. Grateful for the distraction, Nathan watched as his brother stepped out of the house. Talking to Jake would help him get his mind off of Amanda. Hopefully. His thoughts were crowded with her....

God, the taste of her. The scent of her. The feel of her body aligning with his and the hush of her breath on his skin—*damn it.*

Jake leaned against one of the porch posts and asked, "Late night?"

"A few things to see to," he answered vaguely and headed toward the main house.

Jake came down the steps, holding a beer in each hand. He was as tall as Nathan, but where Nathan was broad and muscled, Jake was wiry. His dark brown hair was a little too long, his jeans were worn and faded and his boots were as scarred and scuffed as Nathan's own. He was slow and steady and more at ease with himself and his world than Nathan had ever been.

Jake went his own way and managed to have

a good time while he was doing it. Nathan had always admired that trait in his younger brother.

With a wide grin, Jake handed over one of the frosty bottles. Grateful, Nathan accepted it and took a long drink. When Jake wandered off, Nathan followed his brother across the yard toward the swing set. Apparently, Jake wanted to talk—away from the house. But nothing would get Jake talking before he was good and ready, so Nathan just enjoyed the night and the returning sanity now that he was a safe distance from Amanda.

He'd thought he was well and truly over her. Nathan had deliberately put her out of his mind years ago. He'd lost himself in work and in the arms of the willing women who'd come and gone from his life without leaving so much as a trace of themselves behind. So yeah, he'd figured with Amanda back in town, he'd face her down and keep moving on.

But the hard ache in his body let him know that though his mind had let her go, the rest of him hadn't. And there she was again, he thought in disgust. Right back in his thoughts, front and center. He closed his mind to the memories and focused on the now.

There were a few dawn-to-dusk lights around the play area and he took a second or two to look it over. He and Jake had dug out the wide area beneath the playground equipment and then poured enough fine sand to sink an aircraft carrier. It had taken the two of them nearly two weeks to get everything set up and finished off for safety, but knowing his niece and nephews loved it made all the work worth the effort.

Made of sanded, polished wood—to prevent splinters in tiny hands—the climbing gym sprawled across the pristine lawn as if it had grown in that spot. Jake's five-year-old twin sons and their two-year-old sister loved climbing on it and especially enjoyed the castle-like room at the top. Gave him a good feeling, seeing the next generation of Battles clambering all over the structure, hooting and hollering at each other, just like he and Jake had done when they were kids. It also made him remember that if things had turned out differently, his own child might have been playing here as well.

He shook off that disquieting thought and buried it under another long drink of his beer.

Jake slapped one hand against the swing set and blurted, “So, how’s Amanda?”

Nathan almost choked on his swallow of beer. When the coughing ended and he could breathe again, he looked at his younger brother. “How the hell did you know I went to see her?”

Jake shrugged. “Mona Greer was walking that tiny excuse for a dog of hers and saw you going into the diner apartment. She called Sarah Danvers, Sarah talked to her daughter and Amelia called Terri a while ago.”

The Royal hotline was already buzzing.

“Well, hell,” he muttered. So much for keeping his private life private. He hadn’t seen a damn soul around the diner. Mona Greer should look into a career with the CIA or something. Even at eighty, her eyesight was damn good and she clearly had a sneaky streak.

Jake laughed. “Seriously? You thought you could slide in and out of Amanda’s apartment and nobody would catch on?”

“A man can dream,” Nathan mumbled.

Jake laughed even louder and Nathan told himself there was nothing more irritating sometimes than a younger brother. "Did you come out here just to bushwhack me with gossip then laugh at me?"

"Of course," his brother said with a good-natured shrug. "Not every day I get to give you grief over something."

"Glad you're enjoying yourself."

"Yeah? Well, *I'm* glad to see Amanda back. Glad to see it bugs you."

"Thanks for the support," Nathan told him and took a drink of his beer. His gaze moved over the play equipment. In the moonlight, the slide gleamed like a river of silver and the pennant flag on the castle top fluttered in the hot Texas wind.

Irritation swelled inside him. Three years he'd been sheriff. He had respect. He had the admiration of the townspeople. Now, he was just grist for the mill.

"You want support? Go back to the TCC and talk to Chance. Or Alex." Jake toasted him with his beer. "From family, you get the truth, whether you want it or not."

"I don't." Nathan leaned against one of the posts as visions of Amanda roared into his brain again. He shouldn't have gone to her. But how could he not have? They'd had to talk. But then, there hadn't only been *talking,* had there?

"I know you don't want to hear it but you're going to anyway." Jake paused, ran one hand over the heavy chain from which one of the swings hung. "So here it is. You missed your chance with Amanda back in the day."

Nathan snorted. "I didn't miss a thing. Trust me."

Shaking his head, Jake said, "You know what I mean. You let her get away."

"I didn't *let* her do a damn thing, Jake," Nathan said tightly as he pushed away from the heavy wooden post. "Her decision to walk."

Jake was unaffected by the anger in Nathan's voice. "Right. And you didn't try to talk her out of it."

"Why the hell should I have?" Stalking off a few paces, Nathan's boots slid in the sand he and his brother had laid beneath the swing set. This was his place. The home he'd grown up in. The town where he'd carved out a spot for himself. Damned if he'd let the past jump up and ruin what he'd built.

At the far end of the play equipment, Nathan turned to look at his brother. Jake looked relaxed…amused, damn him.

Well, why wouldn't he be? Jake had everything he'd ever wanted. He ran the ranch. He was married to his high school sweetheart and they had three great kids plus another on the way. Everything was riding smooth in Jake's world—not that Nathan begrudged his brother's happiness. But at the same time, you'd think Jake could manage a little sympathy.

"I'm not going to *beg* a woman to stay with me."

"Who said anything about *begging?*" Jake shot back. "You could have asked."

"No," Nathan said, shaking his head and looking away from his brother's too-sharp eyes to stare out over the moonlit lawn. "I couldn't. There were…reasons."

Reasons he'd never talked about. Never even mentioned to Jake, and Nathan was closer to his brother than to anyone else on the planet. Those reasons tried to push into his mind now and Nathan resolutely pushed them out again. He'd dealt with them all years ago. He wouldn't go back, damn it.

"You listened to the gossip. You believed the rumors instead of talking to Amanda about them."

His head snapped up and his gaze locked on his brother like a twin pair of dark brown lasers. "What do you know about the rumors?"

Jake took a sip of his beer. "Chance told me what was going on—" He held up one hand to keep his brother quiet. "And don't blame him for it. You sure as hell didn't bother to tell me. You're my brother, Nate. You could have said something."

He shook his head and squelched the burst of anger struggling to come alive inside him. "I didn't want to talk about it then—" He paused and added for emphasis, "I still don't."

He didn't like remembering those days. Remembering how he'd felt when Chance told him what people were saying. Nathan had been in the police academy in Houston, unable to get to Amanda. Hell, he hadn't even had time for a damn phone call. And when he had finally been able to go to her…

Shaking his head, Nathan mentally closed the door on the past. It was done and he wouldn't be revisiting it anytime soon.

"You always were the hardhead in the family," Jake said on a sigh.

Nathan managed a short laugh at that. "Seems to me your Terri might argue with you there."

"Probably," Jake admitted with a wince. "Nate, I don't know what happened between you two seven years ago—" he held up a hand again "—and I'm not asking. I'm just saying, she's home to stay now and you're going to have to find a way to get past whatever happened so long ago. You're going to have to deal with her. Maybe the two of you should actually try talking about what happened to break you guys up."

Nathan grimaced, took a pull at his beer and let the icy froth cool down the temper that was still simmering inside him. "Where is all this talking, share-your-feelings stuff coming from? Is Terri making you watch Dr. Phil again?"

"No." Jake looked embarrassed. "But I'm not an idiot any more than you are and I *know* you know you have to make your peace with Amanda."

Another sip of ice-cold beer slid down Nathan's throat as he thought about what his brother said. And then a fresh memory of Amanda, molding her body to his. The heat of her kiss. The scent of her filled his mind. The feel of her beneath his hands again. His body stirred and he winced at the ache that he had a feeling was going to become all too familiar.

"Jake," Nathan said softly, "you don't get it. I learned a long time ago, where Amanda's concerned, there *is* no peace."

# Four

One thing Amanda had always loved about living in Royal was the big farmers' market held every weekend in the park.

Ranchers and farmers from all over the county showed up to sell fresh vegetables, fruit and preserves. There were always craft booths as well, with local artisans selling everything from jewelry to ceramics and handmade toys.

At barely 9:00 a.m., the sun was already a hot ball of misery glowering down on the town. By afternoon, the only people not huddled in an air-conditioned room would be the kids. But for right now, the park was buzzing with activity. The busiest vendors in the park were those who had claimed a spot beneath the shade of a live oak.

Amanda had the day off and she was determined to enjoy it. But, as she wandered through the market, it was clear that the Royal rumor mill was in high gear.

She felt the speculative glances thrown her way as she passed and she lifted her chin defiantly in response. No point in hiding, she told herself. Instead, she would just ignore the fact that whispered conversations would stop when she got close and pick up again as she moved off. Clearly, *someone* had seen Nathan at her place the other night and it hadn't taken long for tongues to start wagging.

Amanda stopped at a booth displaying hand-thrown pottery and idly picked up a kiln-fired, sky-blue pitcher.

The artist, a young woman with waist-length blond hair and bright green eyes, smiled at her. "I'm running a special today on the cornflower-blue pottery."

And if she'd picked up one of the earthenware jugs, Amanda thought, *that* would have been the special of the day. But she couldn't blame the woman for doing her best to make a sale. Besides, she was going to be looking for a house in town soon and she'd need to furnish it, wouldn't she? Smiling, she said, "It's lovely work. How much?"

"Only thirty-five."

"Sold," Amanda told her and set the pitcher down to reach for her wallet. She probably could have haggled, but it was beautiful and she really did want it.

Purchase made, Amanda left a satisfied artist behind her, tucked her new pitcher into the cloth shopping bag slung over her shoulder and wandered off toward the next booth.

"Amanda, hi!" Piper Kindred waved her over with a wide grin. Piper's curly red hair was drawn back into a ponytail and her green eyes were shining. "Haven't had a chance to talk to you since you moved back home."

"I know. Things have been so busy, but we have got to get together soon." Amanda had known Piper most of her life and seeing her friend now made Amanda realize again how much she'd missed being a part of Royal.

"I hear you and Nathan are getting cozy again…"

"Of course you did," Amanda said. A few days ago, Nathan had shown up at her apartment and kissed her senseless. Ever since then, she'd had dozens of customers who spent most of their time at the diner watching *her.* Including Nathan, she reminded herself. He made time to come in at least once a day. He'd order coffee, sit at the counter and watch her as she moved around the room.

Nerve-racking on all fronts.

"Anything you care to share?" Piper teased.

"Not a thing," Amanda assured her old friend, then abruptly changed the subject. "So," she asked, stepping back to read the sign strung across the front of the booth Piper was manning, "what're you selling?"

"Raffle tickets," Piper told her and used her thumb to fan a stack of them. "We're raising money to help pay for the new child-care center at the TCC."

Grinning, Amanda said, "I heard the motion passed. Beau Hacket must have been purple with fury."

"By all reports," Piper assured her. Then she sighed. "I only wish I'd seen it myself. You remember Shannon Morrison? She tells me she came within a breath of hog-tieing the old coot just for the hell of it."

Beau was possibly the last living true chauvinist in the world. He liked women fine, as long as they stayed in their "place." Amanda had never been able to figure out why a woman as nice as his wife, Barbara, had married the man in the first place. "Sorry I missed it."

"More and more women are becoming members of the TCC now that Abby Price paved the way." Piper paused. "I'm not a member or anything, but I wanted to help with this raffle. How many tickets are you going to buy?"

Shaking her head, Amanda reached for her wallet and laughed. "Give me five."

"Atta girl." Piper peeled off the tickets and waited while Amanda wrote her name and phone number on the stubs. When she was finished, Piper dropped the stubs into a steel box and said, "The draw's in a week. Who knows? You might win the grand prize."

"What is it?"

"A weekend getaway in Dallas." Piper shrugged. "Personally, I'd rather win the free dinner at Claire's."

"Hey," Amanda countered, in a mocking insulted tone, "how about you come eat at the diner instead? We've got lemon meringue pie tomorrow."

"Now you're talking," Piper said. "I'll come in around lunch. Maybe we can sit and talk over pie. You can give me the real story behind the gossip."

"You'll be disappointed. There is no story." Except for that kiss, Amanda thought. She waved a goodbye, then moved on. She was still smiling when she caught the scent of fresh-brewed coffee along with a delectable aroma of cinnamon coming from nearby. Marge Fontenot had probably brought in her homemade cinnamon rolls to sell in the coffee booth her husband ran. Amanda's stomach growled in anticipation as she headed for the vendor cart with the long line snaking in front of it.

"Doing some shopping?"

She stopped and looked at Alex Santiago as he approached her.

"I am." As the sun shone down on her, she was grateful she'd tucked her hair into a ponytail that morning. But Alex looked cool and comfortable in khaki slacks and a short-sleeved white shirt. "Living in the city, I really missed farmers' market days."

His gaze swept across the crowded park. "I admit, I enjoy them as well. Last week I bought a new pair of boots…."

She glanced down and nodded in approval at the hand-tooled brown leather boots he wore. "Very nice."

"Thank you. And just now, I've purchased what I am told is the—" he paused to reach into a paper bag and draw out a jar long enough to read the label "—world's best huckleberry jam." He shrugged and gave her a smile that could probably melt ice at a hundred yards.

Amanda just chuckled. "If you bought that jam from Kaye Cannarozzi, I guarantee it *is* the world's best. She's won prizes for her jam every year at the state fair."

"Good to know," he said and folded up the bag again. "You can find just about anything here, I've discovered."

Amanda watched him as he looked around the park. He was dark and gorgeous and his accent made every word sound like seduction. Alex was also nice, funny and, except for his dubious taste in friends—Nathan for example—he was pretty much perfect. Too bad for Amanda that the only bell he rung for her was one of friendship.

"Hmm," Alex mused. "I'm curious as to what put a frown on your face just then. Dark thoughts?"

She forced a smile and shook her head. "Not at all. Um, I'm headed for the coffee wagon over there." She pointed and asked, "Would you like to join me?"

"I could use some coffee as well, so, yes." He fell into step beside her. "I'm looking forward to the Fourth of July celebration. I hear it's quite the event."

"Oh, it's great," Amanda told him. "Most of the town gathers right here for an all-day party. There are contests and games and the fireworks show is always amazing. If I do say so myself, we put on a terrific Fourth."

Funny how good it felt to say *we.*

"Sounds as though you've missed it."

"I really did," she admitted, glancing around the park at the people wandering from booth to booth. Kids raced away from their parents, laughing as they headed to the playground. Dogs on leashes strained against their owners' restraining hands and a hot summer wind kicked up out of nowhere.

Royal was home. There was no other place like it and she'd never really been happy anywhere else. "You know, I told myself while I was gone that I was fine. That life in the city was better, somehow. But now that I'm back, it's like I never left."

"Going home isn't always possible," he mused. "I'm glad you're finding it easier than you'd thought."

Amanda looked up at him and saw that while his stare was fixed on the distance, a slight frown was etched into his features. She didn't know Alex well, but she sensed something was bothering him. Before she could offer to help, though, he spoke again.

"I'm pleased to see that the gossip hasn't upset you."

She sighed. The downside to small-town life. She'd already had several people stop her in the park that morning, asking questions, giving her sly winks and knowing smiles. Nathan and she were the talk of the town and until something really juicy came up, that wasn't going to change.

"You've heard it, too?"

He gave her a rueful grin. "I think you would have to be on the moon to miss it."

"Know anyone who could give me a ride?"

"Sadly, no." He shrugged and added, "Though a beautiful woman shouldn't let loose talk from small minds worry her."

Amanda stopped, cocked her head and looked up at him. "You really *are* perfect, aren't you?"

His mouth quirked. "I like to think so, though I'm sure others would disagree."

"Not from where I'm standing."

"For that, I thank you. Besides, gossip isn't

a static thing, Amanda," he said. "Very soon, they'll find something else to talk about."

"I suppose," she said, looking at the crowds in the park. Most of the people she'd known her whole life. Oh, there were plenty of outsiders who had come into town solely for market day. But the great majority were familiar to her. Which was probably why everyone felt free enough to talk about her.

She knew they were watching her now, too. Wondering why she was walking with Alex when it was clear she and Nathan were starting up again. A tiny twist of pain wrapped itself around her heart. "As much as I love Royal, it's not always an easy place to live."

"No place is easy," Alex said, his expression becoming thoughtful again, as if there were things chewing at him.

Somehow, she'd struck a nerve, Amanda thought. From what she knew, Alex Santiago hadn't been in town very long and she wondered if anyone really knew him well. Reaching out, she threaded her arm companionably through his. "Everything okay, Alex?"

Immediately, his handsome face brightened as he flashed her a smile. “You’ve a kind heart Amanda, but there’s no need for concern. I’m fine.”

“Am I interrupting?”

Amanda looked up when Nathan’s deep voice demanded her attention. He was only a few feet away, headed right for her. The sunlight winked off the sheriff’s badge pinned to his broad chest. He wore his favorite scuffed boots and a uniform shirt tucked into black jeans. The gun at his hip made him look even more formidable than usual. His gaze was fixed on hers, but still he managed to fire a brief glare at Alex.

A flash of heat shot through Amanda at Nathan’s nearness and made the heat of the summer sun seem no hotter than a match-head in comparison. She wanted to fan herself, but she knew it wouldn’t do any good, so she settled for sarcastic indifference instead.

“If I said ‘yes you are,’” Amanda quipped, “would you go away?”

His eyes flashed. “Not until I know what you guys are talking about.”

Alex grinned at his friend. “About small towns and smaller minds.”

Nathan frowned and nodded. “You mean the gossip.”

“Among other things,” Amanda said, drawing Nathan’s eyes back to her. She knew him so well she could see the tension in his face. The gossip was irritating to her. To Nathan, it had to be infuriating. “What do you want, Nathan?”

“Coffee, one of Margie’s cinnamon rolls and to talk to you. Not necessarily in that order.”

So, there wasn’t even going to be a pretense of friendliness between them. He was acting as if the kiss they’d shared hadn’t happened. As if putting it out of his mind made the whole scene disappear.

“I’m busy,” she said. “Alex and I are shopping.”

She should have known that men would stick together. Alex immediately said, “Actually, there are a few things I have to take care of. I’ve enjoyed myself, Amanda.” Shifting his gaze to his friend, he nodded and said, “I’ll see you later, Nathan.”

“You don’t have to go,” Amanda told him

quickly. Without Alex there, she and Nathan wouldn't have a buffer. And she suddenly wanted one really badly.

"Yeah, you do," Nathan said at the same time.

Alex only laughed. "You two are very entertaining. I'll be on my way."

Around them, conversations rose and fell. A sultry wind teased the hem of her shorts and in the distance, children played and laughed. Amanda knew that she and Nathan were now the center of attention, but she didn't care anymore. Alex had been right about one thing. Sooner or later, everyone would find a new topic of interest. Until then, her best choice was simply to ignore them all. People would talk and she couldn't stop them. So instead, she continued on toward Margie's coffee cart and wasn't surprised to have Nathan right at her side.

"Mona Greer saw me at your place when I was there a few nights ago," he told her, his voice low and deep.

"Well, that explains a few things," Amanda said wryly.

"That woman should have been a spy."

"Maybe she was. Now she's retired," Amanda mused, "and she's looking for new things to occupy her."

He snorted a short laugh. "That'd be something. Mona in the CIA."

Amanda laughed, too, then Nathan looked down at her and she caught the confusion in his eyes.

"This doesn't bother you? Being talked about?" Nathan asked.

"A little," she admitted. "Okay, a lot. But I can't stop it, so why make myself nuts?"

"Healthy attitude."

"I try," she said, and fell into line at the coffee cart.

Nathan stayed beside her and, keeping his voice low, he said, "I still think we need to set some ground rules, Amanda."

"Like you coming around the diner to keep an eye on me?"

He frowned.

"Or are you talking about when you kissed me?"

She had the satisfaction of seeing a flash of

temper spark in his eyes. Then he spoke as if she hadn't said a thing. "We agree that there's nothing between us anymore and—"

Amanda didn't have to speak. She only looked up at him, making no attempt at all to hide the smile curving her mouth. Nothing between them? Hadn't they proven just the other night that if nothing else, there was still plenty of heat between them?

He scowled, clearly understanding what she wasn't saying. Then he muttered, "That doesn't count."

"Felt like it counted to me." In fact, that one kiss had kept her awake most of the night feeling restless, edgy. Memories had crowded in on her until all she could think about was Nathan and how things used to be between them. That kiss had stirred up everything for her, making the last few days really uncomfortable. And now Nathan wanted to pretend it hadn't happened?

Nathan looked down at her and watched her meadow-green eyes narrow. She was mad. He liked that. Better than amused. Or accepting.

Anger was safer. For both of them. Except for the fact that she looked so damn good when she was pissed off at him. Gave her a fire he'd never found in any other woman.

Her light brown hair was pulled into a high ponytail at the back of her head. She wore gold hoops in her ears that dangled long enough to skim her smooth shoulders, displayed nicely in a navy blue tank top. Her white shorts showed off her tan and made her legs look as if they were a mile long, and the sandals let him see she still wore the gold toe ring he'd given her on her left foot.

A breeze sent her ponytail dancing and it was all Nathan could do to keep from reaching up and twining that silky mass around his fingers. Damn it, she was in him again. As fiercely as she had been years ago. For days now, he'd been tormented by thoughts of her. By memories so thick they'd nearly choked him. He'd hardly slept for dreams of her and when he woke, it was to a body that was hard and aching for want of her.

His talk with Jake hadn't helped any. He'd meant it when he said there was no peace with

Amanda. But back in the day he hadn't been looking for peace, had he? All he'd been able to think about was her. Her laugh. Her eyes. Her scent. Her taste. The feel of her hands on his body and the sweet brush of her breath when she kissed him.

Hell, no, that wasn't peaceful.

It was…consuming.

And it was happening again. Only this time, he'd come up with a plan to combat it. It had hit him in the shower just that morning—another damn cold one—that what he needed to do was get Amanda back in his bed.

Over the years, Nathan had convinced himself that he'd idealized what he and Amanda had shared. That was why he hadn't been able to find another woman to compare to her. His own mind had set him up for failure by making the memories of Amanda so amazing that what woman *could* hold a candle to her?

What was needed here was a little reality. And sex was the key. Get her in his bed, and get her out of his mind once and for all.

It was the only road to sanity.

Once he'd had her again, he could let her go. This tension between them would finally be over.

As his plan settled into his mind, he smiled to himself.

"What?" Amanda asked.

"What do you mean?"

"You're smiling," she pointed out.

"And that's bad?" He laughed a little and moved forward as the line continued to snake ahead.

"Not bad," Amanda said, still watching him warily. "Just…suspicious."

Behind them in line, someone chuckled.

Nathan frowned. Damned hard to work on seducing a woman when you had half the town watching your every move. "So when I'm angry, you're mad and when I'm not, you're worried."

She thought about it for a second, then nodded. "That's about right."

For just a moment, Nathan enjoyed the confusion in her eyes and found himself laughing briefly. "There really is no one else like you, is there?"

"Probably not," she admitted and moved a bit closer to the head of the line.

She could always drive him out of his mind, Nathan thought, letting his gaze move over her in appreciation. He'd always liked tall women—they were right in easy kissing range. Amanda, though, was like no one else. Or at least that's how he remembered it. Even in high school, when she was a freshman and he a senior, he'd been drawn to her. His friends had given him grief over it, of course—but he hadn't been able to stay away.

And then, years later, those same friends had told him about the rumors that had eventually torn him and Amanda apart.

"So tell me, Nathan," she said, shattering his thoughts and drawing him back to the moment, "are you interested in my sister?"

"What?" He goggled at her. "Where did that come from?"

She shrugged, glared at the man behind them, openly listening to their conversation, then leaned in closer to Nathan to say, "I've seen the way she watches you."

Nathan thought about that for a minute. He hadn't noticed Pam looking at him in any particular way. Okay, yes, he'd dated her a couple times a year or so ago, but it hadn't gone anywhere and they'd parted friends. Or he'd thought they had. Until now. Frowning slightly, he said, "We went out a few times a while back, but—"

Her eyes went wide. "I can't believe you dated my *sister,*" she said, cutting him off sharply.

The man behind them in line let out a long, slow whistle, but when Nathan gave him a hard look, the guy got quiet fast.

"It was a couple of dates. Dinner." He thought back. "A movie."

"It was *my sister.*" She fisted her hands at her hips. "How would you like it if I dated Jake?"

"I think his wife would mind it even more than I would."

"You know what I mean."

"Yeah, I do. But we were over, remember?" Nathan whispered and moved with the line. How long *was* this line, anyway? And were there even more people crowded around them than there had been a few minutes ago? "Besides, Pam was here and—"

"So she was *here,*" Amanda said, interrupting

him again and making Nathan grind his teeth together in frustration. "Well, then. Of course I can understand that. The whole proximity factor."

The whistler behind them chuckled now and only shrugged when Nathan gave him another hard stare. This conversation was going to be all over town by suppertime, he told himself, and still he couldn't keep from saying, "At least Pam never lied to me."

She sucked in a gulp of air and her eyes shone with fury. "*Lie* to you? I never lied to you. You were the one who—"

"That's it," he muttered and grabbed hold of her arm.

He wasn't going to do this with a couple dozen people watching them with all the avid interest of a crowd at a football game.

Dragging her out of the line, he headed toward the nearest deserted spot. A shade tree close to the now-empty baseball diamond. Naturally, nothing with Amanda came easy. She tugged and pulled, trying to get out of his grip, but no way was he letting her go until they had this settled. And for this talk, they needed some damn privacy.

"Let go of me!" She kicked at him, but missed.

"In a minute," he muttered.

"I want my coffee. I do *not* want to go anywhere with you."

"That's too damn bad," Nathan told her and never slowed down. When they finally reached the shade of the oak, he let her go and she stared up at him, furious.

"I don't know who you think you are, but—"

"You know exactly who I am," he told her, voice low and filled with the temper crouched inside him. "Just like you know that I hate putting on a show for the whole damn town."

"Fine." She lifted her chin, met him glare for glare and then said, "You want to talk, here it is. I never lied to you, Nathan."

"And I'm supposed to take your word for that?"

"Damn right, you are," she shouted, obviously not caring who was listening. "When did I *ever* give you a reason to *not* trust me, Nathan?"

She had a point, but he didn't want to admit to it. All he remembered were the rumors she hadn't been able to disprove. The sympathetic glances from his friends. The gossip that insisted on a completely different story than the one she'd told him. And his doubts had chewed on him until, ragged with temper and tension, he'd faced her down and in one night, they had lost everything.

"What was I supposed to think?" he demanded. "My best friends told me that story. Why wouldn't I believe them?"

Shaking her head, she looked at him now with more hurt than fury and that tore at him.

"Because you were supposed to *love* me. You should have taken my word for it."

Shame rippled through him and was gone an instant later. He'd done what he thought was right. Hell, he'd been half-crazed back then anyway. When he heard she had lost the baby, he was enrolled in the police academy in Dallas and hadn't been able to get to her. Hadn't even been able to call her. To figure out truth from lies.

"It was a long time ago, Amanda."

"Was it?" she asked quietly. "Doesn't feel like it right now."

No, it didn't. The past was there, in the park

with them. Shadows of memories crowded together, dimming the sunlight, making the other people in the park fade away until it was just he and Amanda. He looked into her eyes and said, "All right then. Tell me now. The truth."

She sighed. "I shouldn't have to tell you again, Nathan. You know me. You knew me then. You should have believed me. I *lost* our baby."

Pain slapped at him but he pushed it away. Now that the past was here, it was time to finally settle it. If he wanted to get her out of his mind, then he was going to have to make a start right here.

"Then who the hell was it who made sure I thought you had *ended* the pregnancy on purpose?"

# Five

"I don't know," Amanda said, shaking her head. She still couldn't believe anyone had spread that rumor. Couldn't believe that Nathan had thought for even a minute that she would ever do such a thing.

In a flash, Amanda was back there, on the night when everything crashed down around her. They'd been engaged for two weeks—because Nathan had insisted on a wedding the moment he found out she was pregnant. But that night, she had been the one doing the insisting.

*"The wedding's off, Nathan."*

*"Just like that?"*

*"The only reason you were marrying me was because of the baby, right?" Those words cost her. She so wanted him to say that wasn't true. That he loved her. Always had. That they would be okay, they would get past this.*

*But he didn't.*

*And she couldn't marry a man who didn't love her—no matter how much she loved him.*

*"So that's it?" he demanded. "Now that you're not pregnant, you don't need me anymore, that it? Find someone richer?"*

*Stunned, she could only look at him. She had never cared a damn about his money. She'd loved him for as long as she could remember. And she'd convinced herself that he cared for her, too. Even though he'd never actually said the words. Now she could see she'd been living in a dream world. "How can you say that?"*

*"Oh, I'm not done," he told her flatly. "You said you lost the baby, but that's not the whole story, is it?"*

*Amanda stared up at him. She had expected him to be supportive. To share the pain that was still tearing through her. The loss of the baby, her hopes, her dreams for the future. They were all gone now.*

*She'd needed Nathan so badly. Now that he was here, she only wanted him gone.*

*"I don't know what you mean," she said finally.*

*"Yeah, I think you do." He stalked around the perimeter of her tiny Midland apartment. "Hell, you hated the thought of marrying me so much you got rid of my baby?"*

*"What?" Shock held her in place. Outrage made her want to scream. Pain held her in such a tight grip she could hardly breathe. "You think—"*

*"Thought I wouldn't find out, didn't you?" he asked, his voice dripping with ice.*

*"There was nothing to find out, Nathan." Through her pain, anger began to blossom like a black rose. She gave it free rein. "I lost the baby. I had a miscarriage. I told you."*

*He scrubbed one hand across the top of his head. "Yeah, that's what you told me. Others told me something different."*

*"And you'd believe them? Believe that I could do something like that to our child?"*

*His eyes were hard, his expression distant, remote. "Why would anyone say that if it wasn't true?"*

*Good question, but that was for later. Right now, the most important question on her mind was how could he think for even a second that it was true?*

*"How do I know?"*

*"Exactly," he said. "How do I know what to believe, either?"*

*"I guess you have to trust me," she said, knowing he didn't. Knowing he wouldn't.*

*"Yeah." His eyes were as cold as the moon. Suddenly he looked like a stranger to her and Amanda knew she wouldn't be able to reach him because he didn't want to be reached.*

*So much lost, all in a blink of time. She swayed with the impact of what was happening.*

*He turned and walked to the door. There, he stopped and looked back at her. "You're right about one thing, though. The wedding's off. I was only marrying you because of the baby. With the reason gone, there's no point, is there?"*

*The fact that his words echoed what she had*

*thought herself only moments before just made the pain that much deeper. Sharper. When Nathan left, the quiet click of the door shutting behind him sounded like a gunshot. It seemed to echo in the empty room long after he'd left her. Long after Amanda had curled up on the couch to cry herself to sleep.*

Shaking her head as if she could somehow dislodge the painful memories, Amanda looked up at him through eyes that were no longer starry with love for a man who refused to love her back. She wasn't young and foolish anymore. If she still loved Nathan, that was her problem and she'd find a way to get over it. But he would never know that he still had so much power over her heart.

"You walked out, Nathan," she reminded him in a voice that was low and throbbing with remembered hurt.

"Yeah," he admitted, "I did. But you were the one to end things between us. Hell, I walked in the door and you handed me the ring."

"You agreed with me about calling off the wedding," she reminded him.

"Damn straight, I did. You weren't pregnant. You'd already handed me the ring—"

"You wouldn't *talk* to me," she said.

"You didn't give me a chance to say anything and even if you had, what the hell could I say?" he countered. "It was done. The baby was gone and your ring was in my fist. What do you think I should have said, for God's sake?"

"That you believed me." That was the one thing that had always stung. He had known her better than anyone else—or so she had thought. And he'd taken the word of malicious gossips over her.

How was she supposed to forget that?

He scrubbed both hands across his face as memories crowded so close he could hardly draw a breath. The rumors had driven him crazy when he couldn't get to her. At first, she was in the hospital and then when she was out, he was confined to the academy. Couldn't even talk to her. Couldn't look into her eyes and see for himself truth from lies. But by the time he finally reached her side, the crazy had taken over. The doubts. The disappointment and fury had him so tangled into knots it was all he could do to hold it together.

Hell, he prided himself on control. On being in charge of every damn thing around him. He had his own personal rules of conduct. And he'd blown them all on that long-ago night. Duty. Honor. They'd both gone out the window when anger made him blind to common sense.

Blowing out a breath, he stared up at the sky for a long minute, then lowered his gaze to hers. Doubts still gnawed at the edges of his heart, but being with her, looking into her eyes, clouded with hurt, he could see the truth that had eluded him for so long. "I do believe you."

The moment he said it, he knew it was right. Back then, he'd been young and stupid. He'd wanted her to rush into his arms looking for comfort. He'd wanted her to cry and mourn their lost child so he would *know* that she hadn't ended her pregnancy. Instead, she'd handed him the ring he'd given her and told him, more or less, to move on.

So his own self-assurance took a hit and then delivered one right back. Hurt, he'd made sure that she hurt, too. He wasn't saying he was right. He was only saying—screw it.

A sheen of tears filmed the brilliant green of her eyes, but before he could panic or kick his own ass for making her cry, she blinked them back. She took a breath, steadied herself and said, "Thanks for that, anyway. Better late than never, huh?"

"I guess," he said, but this conversation still felt unfinished.

She hitched her bag higher on her shoulder. "Now, I've got to go."

"Damn it, Amanda—don't walk away."

"What else is there to talk about, Nathan? We're over and done, and standing here in the park together is only going to fire up the gossip train you hate."

True.

He did hate knowing that, but there didn't seem to be much he could do about it. For days now, he'd lived with everyone in town watching his every move. With having people drop by the jailhouse for a "friendly chat" when what they were really looking for was more grist for the rumor mill. They wanted exclusive news about Nathan and Amanda so *they* could be the ones to spill the next part of the story.

Hell, he was actually getting used to it.

He'd come here today, knowing the gossips were chewing on them, knowing that meeting her like this would only make things worse. But this was his plan. Talk with her, bed her, then move on and—damn it—he was going to stick to it. It was a good plan, even if it had gotten more involved than he'd originally thought it would.

Nathan hadn't meant to dig into the past. Hadn't intended to throw up that night between them like a damn battle flag. He didn't want her pissed—despite how good she looked when fire was in her eyes. He didn't want her sad. Or resigned.

He wanted her hot and ready and as eager to be with him as he was to get his hands on her. But he couldn't do that until he ended the war.

"You're off tonight, right?"

"What?" She looked as surprised as he was over his blurted question.

Taking hold of her arm again, he drew her

around to the far side of the old oak, using the tree to block most people's views of them.

"Let go, Nathan."

He did, though his fingers still felt the warmth of her skin long after he drew his hand back. Through the years, through the old pain and shared memories, the heat between them lingered. He was more convinced than ever that he was doing the right thing. Get her back into bed, feel the burn again so that he could finally let it—and her—go.

"We need some time, Amanda," he said, keeping his gaze locked with hers. "Time to talk. To find a way to be in this town together."

She was shaking her head so he talked faster, refusing to give her enough room to back away. "Come out with me tonight. We'll have dinner—and time."

"I don't know…."

Confusion etched itself onto her features. He could see her weighing her decision, so he gave her a little push. "Not afraid to be alone with me, are you?"

It worked.

Her head snapped up and she snorted. “Afraid? Please.”

He grinned. “Then it’s settled.”

“Fine.” She nodded at him. “Where do you want to meet?”

“I’ll pick you up at your place about seven.”

She laughed a little uneasily. “This is Saturday. Everyone for miles around will be in town. You’re not worried about how many people will see us together?”

He glanced up at the crowd milling around the park before looking back to her. What was the point of hiding now? They were already the center of every conversation in town. No sense trying to fight it. “They’re already talking, remember? Besides, damned if I’m going to sneak around.”

She nodded. “Good point.”

“All right, then. See you at seven.”

Over at the diner, Pam leaned on the counter and tapped her fingernails against it in a sharp staccato. “People have been talking about them all day.”

"You shouldn't be listening."

"How can I not?" She shook her head and gave a quick look around at the people sitting at the booths and counters. Peggy, the other waitress on duty, was laughing with her customers and in the kitchen behind her, Pam could hear the cooks talking while they worked. The diner was busy and that was a good thing. The fact that it was all because of Amanda made it harder to appreciate.

"She's been back home for a couple of weeks and she's taking over again."

She looked at the man sitting in front of her. JT McKenna had been her friend since school. He ran his own ranch just outside of town where he raised a small herd of cattle and his pride and joy, quarter horses.

His dark brown hair curled over the collar of his shirt and his tanned face showed a line of white across the top of his forehead where his hat normally rested. He was tall and lean and according to Pam's friends, gorgeous. She'd never really noticed because JT had always been just her friend.

Now, he cupped his hands around a cup of coffee and shook his head. "Pam, you're the one who asked her to come home."

She sighed. Hard to admit, but he was right. Pam had tried to run the diner on her own, but it just hadn't worked. She'd been overwhelmed with trying to handle the whole place on her own. But she still hated to acknowledge that Amanda had made a difference. Her younger sister had always been the golden one. Her parents' favorite. Taller, smarter, prettier… Pam's fingernails sounded out like a jackhammer.

It wasn't that she didn't like her sister. But did Amanda have to be so perfect?

"You're getting wound up over nothing, Pam," JT said.

His brown eyes were on her and she had to sigh. "You're probably right, but—"

"No buts," he teased and gave her a grin that lit up his eyes. "You're so focused on Amanda and Nathan you can't see anything else around you."

"Like what?"

JT blew out a breath and said, "Like I could use some more coffee."

"Oh, sure." She turned to reach for the pot and

told herself she needed to calm down. But the last few days had made that nearly impossible. Everyone was talking about Nathan and Amanda again. Just as they had all those years ago.

Nathan.

Her heart ached at the thought of him. Without even trying, her little sister had even gotten the man Pam had always wanted. All those years when Amanda was living away from Royal, Pam had done everything she could to capture Nathan's attention. But it was as if he was completely oblivious to her. Even the couple of times she'd managed to get him out to dinner and to a movie, nothing had come of it.

"Still," she said thoughtfully, "according to Dora Plant, Nathan and Amanda were arguing at the park today."

"You're doing it again," JT told her flatly. "I can see it in your eyes. You're thinking on how you can get around your sister to Nathan and it's not going to get you anywhere. You best watch your step, and move careful, Pam."

"What?"

"You and Amanda," he said gently, "you're *family.* Always will be."

"I know that—" she argued.

He cut her off. "Maybe you do, but I'm thinking you tend to forget what you don't want to think about. My point is, you should open your eyes, Pam. Nathan's not interested in you that way and probably never will be."

She flushed, but couldn't seem to stop it. Pam had hungered after Nathan for so long, it had become a way of life for her. All the time he was with her sister, that knowledge had eaten away at her like acid. But then the two of them broke up and Pam began to hope again. All right, nothing had come of their few dates, but that didn't mean she should give up.

"You don't know what it's like, JT."

He laughed shortly, shook his head and dug money out of his wallet. Laying the bills on the counter, he said, "You'd be surprised by what I know, Pam."

She watched him go, then turned back to her customers, still wondering what JT had meant.

* * *

A few hours later, Amanda was standing in front of her mirror, trying to figure out how Nathan had maneuvered her into this. She wasn't even sure why she was going along with…what was it? A date? Her stomach swirled at the thought.

"It's not a date," she said, just to hear it said out loud. She dragged a brush through her hair. "It *feels* like a date. It shouldn't, but it does. God, I haven't been on a date in—" She stopped because even if there was no one else there to hear her, admitting out loud that it had been *three years* since she'd been on a real, live, guy-picks-you-up-and-pays date was too humiliating.

No wonder she was nervous.

Music pumped from the radio in the living room and Amanda smiled at herself in the mirror. Looked more like a grimace, but she'd take it. She had no idea where Nathan was taking her, so she'd changed her outfit three times, finally settling on a pale blue skirt that hit just above her knees, a white, short-sleeved blouse that buttoned up the front and a pair of sandals with a heel that would bring her almost to eye level with Nathan.

And there was the swirl of nerves in the pit of her stomach again.

*Notadate...notadate...notadate...*

The chant went through her mind but couldn't seem to find anything to hold on to. Because she'd been off balance ever since she'd returned to Royal. Those first two weeks, waiting to see him again. Then that first meeting in the diner, when he'd been so cold, so remote. Only to have him show up later, right here and, after demanding she leave town, kiss her until her head was spinning.

No wonder she felt as if she were at the center of a madly spinning tornado. She had no sense of direction. Only the instinctive drive to keep her heart intact this time. To become so immune to Nathan and what he could do to her with a glance that she could finally move on. Find a nice man—one who didn't drive her to impossible highs and heartbreaking lows—and build a life. A life with the children she longed for. A life filled with the love she'd lost so long ago.

So *why* then was she putting herself through this not-a-date? Because she wasn't immune to Nathan yet and just maybe a night spent alone with him might start her on that path.

When a knock sounded at her door, she slapped one hand to her abdomen in a futile attempt to quell all the butterflies nestled in there, then told herself to get a grip. To get over Nathan, she was going to need to restrain her natural tendency to go up in flames around him. She walked across the room, deliberately casual, opened the door and nerves slid away to be replaced by something more elemental. More…hazardous, to her already iffy sense of control.

He wore black jeans, a red, button-down long-sleeve shirt open at the collar and the boots that seemed to be a part of him. He gave her a slow, thorough once-over, then an appreciative smile curved his mouth. "You look great."

Fire licked at her insides, but she squashed the flames flat before they could take hold. This wasn't a romantic thing, for heaven's sake. This was just…who knew what it was?

"Thanks." She grabbed her purse from the

nearby table. God, he smelled good. "I'm ready to go."

That smile of his deepened as he turned her toward the stairs. "Always liked that about you, Amanda. None of this make-him-wait stuff." Taking her hand, he led her down the stairs and then to his car, a big, black SUV he'd left parked on the street.

Saturday night was date night in Royal for young and old alike. A lot of the local ranchers came in to treat the family to dinner out. There were shoppers hitting the stores on Main Street and pedestrians, just out watching other people. And she was sure that most of them were avidly watching her and Nathan.

Nothing could have proven to her more completely that he didn't give a damn about the gossips any more than picking her up on a Saturday night for the whole town to see.

To her left, the wide front windows of the diner shone with light and she knew that everyone in there, too, would have a perfect view of her leaving with Nathan.

As if he knew just what she was thinking, he

squeezed her hand briefly and gave her a conspiratorial wink. Her heart clenched—it was almost as if the two of them were a team again. To underline that sensation, his hand around hers felt warm and strong and…right. She nearly stumbled when that thought zipped through her mind.

Thankfully, she recovered quickly, since an older woman with a crown of gray braids wrapped around her head stopped them on the sidewalk.

"Well, now, what might you two be up to on such a nice summer evening?" Hannah Poole was easily seventy-five. Her eyes—shining with glee—were razor-sharp and her nose was practically twitching with interest. If there was a gossip train in Royal, then Miss Hannah was the engineer. There wasn't a thing that went on in town that she didn't know about.

"Hello, Miss Hannah," Amanda said, tugging at Nathan's hand to stop him. "It's nice to see you."

"I'm sure it is, honey," she said as her gaze locked briefly on their joined hands. "Going somewhere, are you?"

"Yes, ma'am, we sure are," Nathan answered, then surprised Amanda by letting go of her hand only long enough to snake one arm around her waist, steering her toward the car. "And if we don't hurry we'll be late."

"Well, I wouldn't want to keep you," the woman said thoughtfully, eyes gleaming. "I've got to get on home, myself. You two young people have fun, now. Good to see the two of you back together again."

"Oh, we're not—" Amanda began.

"Thank you, Miss Hannah," Nathan said over her. "You have a good evening."

He got Amanda settled, stalked around to the driver's side and climbed in.

"Of course she had to get home," Amanda said, watching as Hannah Poole scurried down the sidewalk. Her feet, clad in sensible brown shoes, moved faster than Amanda had ever known them to go.

"What she meant was, she had to get on the phone and tell everyone who wasn't in town tonight that she saw the two of us together."

"Yep."

She turned her head to stare at him. “Doesn’t that bother you?”

“Yep.” He fired up the engine, checked traffic, then pulled out onto Main Street.

“That’s it? Just ‘yep’?” Amanda’s gaze locked on him. In the old days, Nathan would have been rigidly furious to be the center of attention. This Nathan was a stranger. Mysterious. Intriguing. “Who are you and what have you done with Nathan?”

His lips quirked briefly. “What am I supposed to do? Shoot Miss Hannah? Throw her into a jail cell to keep her off the phone?” He shook his head and turned left. “Nope. No way to stop her or anyone else from talking.”

“Did you have a temper transplant?”

Unexpectedly, he glanced at her and grinned. “No, but not a bad idea.”

She was charmed. How could she not be? Not only was this Nathan—the man she’d been in love with since she was fourteen years old—but tonight he was…different. More relaxed. More…approachable.

Which could be risky, her mind warned. Logically, she should pay attention to that warning. Unfortunately, her body was too busy celebrating Nathan's nearness to worry about possible future problems. And that was a whole different problem. She was supposed to be weaning herself from the allure of Nathan and now he'd made it that much more difficult.

Amanda settled back in the car seat, kept her gaze locked on the street in front of them and tried to stifle the sensations already building inside her.

It wasn't easy.

"So where are we going?"

"You still like surprises?" he asked.

"Yes…"

"Then sit back. Won't take but a minute to get there."

That narrowed down the choices. Even if he was taking her to Claire's restaurant, it was clear on the other side of town. But he wasn't headed in that direction, anyway. They'd only driven a mile or so, when Nathan pulled into a familiar parking lot.

"The TCC?" she asked.

"Problem with that?"

"No." She looked at the building that had been a part of town life since long before she was born. Built in the 1900s, it was a huge, rambling, one-story building constructed of dark stone and wood with a tall, slate roof.

She'd been inside a couple of times before—not as a guest, but as a server when her father had catered meetings. She knew the ceilings were high, the furniture and floors were dark and old-world style and the ambiance was loaded with testosterone. Sure, they were allowing female members now, but not many and not without a battle that had made the Alamo look like a playground tussle.

"I've just never—" She caught herself and shrugged. "I'm just…surprised, I guess."

"Why?" Nathan shut off the engine and looked at her. "The dining room's been open to women for years."

"True, but you never took me there before."

"Yeah," he said, "there's a lot of things I didn't do that maybe I should have."

She didn't even know what to say to that. Did

he have the same kind of regrets she had for the way things had ended between them? Nathan was a master at hiding what he was feeling so unless he came right out and said so, she might never know for sure.

"Maybe that's true of both of us." She offered a truce and was pleased to see his smile in response.

"Could be you're right. But for now, let's just say I'm a changed man." He got out of the car and as he walked around the hood to come to her side, Amanda found herself hoping he hadn't changed *too* much.

Over dinner, she realized that she had forgotten just how charming Nathan could be. His gaze fixed on hers, he led their conversation to happier times. To the years before they'd split up in such a crash of emotions.

All around them, the clink of silver against china and the tinkle of crystal became no more than quiet background noise. The people, the servers, seemed to fade away. She had even stopped noticing the hunting trophies on the walls. With Nathan's full attention on her, it was impossible to be aware of anything else.

The dark paneled walls, the soft lighting and the flickering candles on the tables all made for a romantic setting that Amanda wasn't sure how to interpret. She hadn't expected romance, yet it seemed Nathan was determined to give it to her. Why?

And why couldn't she just enjoy it while it lasted?

They talked about old times, without touching on the painful parts. They talked about what each of them had been doing over the last seven years and slowly, began to work into…what? A friendship? No. That was too pale a word for the connection that hummed between them, whether they were acknowledging it or not.

Of course, because they were in a small town where they knew everyone, their dinner wasn't completely private. Several people paused at their table to say hello and Amanda watched as Nathan became what he was: the sheriff. A man respected and trusted by everyone in town, he answered questions patiently and promised a couple of people to look into their problems. He carried power easily and she realized that the last several years had made a difference. He wasn't the young, arrogant man she'd known back then. Oh, he was still cocky, that came across just fine, but there was an underlying thread of patience that the old Nathan had lacked.

It wasn't just him that had changed. The years had left their mark on both of them. They weren't the same people they had been seven years before. And maybe, if faced with the same situation today, they'd each react differently.

Not that it would change anything now, but she couldn't help wondering how things might have been if only they had trusted each other more. *Talked* to each other, rather than reacting to the pain of the moment.

When they finished their meal, Amanda took a moment to glance around at the elegant dining room, filled with TCC members and their guests. No doubt every one of them would be spreading the word about this dinner she and Nathan had shared—but at the moment, she just didn't care.

Seated across the linen-draped table from him

drinking a cup of coffee, Amanda said, "Thank you. For...bringing me here. I had a great time."

"Good." He glanced at their bill, tucked money inside, then set the black leather folder at the edge of the table. Lifting his own coffee cup, he toasted her and said, "So did I, but the night's not over yet."

"Really? What could possibly top that fabulous dinner?"

"Dessert."

She had to laugh. "Nathan, we both passed on dessert, remember?"

"You won't pass on the one I've got in mind," he assured her.

Amanda looked into his eyes and in the dancing candlelight, she read *desire* in those depths. Tingles of something expectant, something amazing, went off like sparklers in the pit of her belly and even lower.

A deep, throbbing ache pounded out inside her to the rhythm of her own heartbeat and the longer she held his gaze, the faster that rhythm became. Here was the danger, she told herself sternly. And if she had a single ounce of common sense, she'd ask him to take her home. Now.

But she knew she wasn't going to do that.

It had been seven long years since she and Nathan had been alone together. Seven years since she'd felt this sizzle of bone-deep attraction. Years since she'd been able to look into those chocolate-brown eyes and see the need she saw now.

No. No matter what happened next, she wouldn't be leaving him. Not yet.

"Well, now I'm intrigued," she managed to say.

"Then let's get going." He stood up and held one hand out to her.

She only hesitated a moment before laying her hand in his and allowing him to draw her to her feet. Their gazes met and in the quiet elegance of the room, it felt as if explosions were going off all around them but only *they* could feel them. If interested gazes followed them as they left, Amanda was oblivious to them.

Nathan led her out of the club, into the warm, moist air of a Texas summer's evening. Wherever they were headed next, she knew there was nowhere else she'd rather be.

# Six

As they drove through town and took a turn in the direction of the Battlelands, Amanda looked at Nathan's profile. There was a slight smile on his face, but that told her nothing other than that he was pleased with himself. *Hmm.*

"Are we going to the ranch house?"

He glanced at her and smiled. "You'll see."

Why was he being so secretive? What was he up to?

She could play along, so she said, "It'd be nice to see Jake and Terri again. Been a long time since I've seen their kids."

"Uh-huh. You will eventually."

So, probably not going there right now. Okay, fine. She could be patient. To a point.

"How're you and Pam getting along these days?"

The question caught her off guard and made her a little uncomfortable at the same time.

"About the same," she said. "She's glad I'm there in the diner, but I think she'd rather if I could phone in the work from somewhere else."

He frowned. "She's got some issues with you."

"There's a news flash," she murmured. She had a couple of issues with Pam, too, now that she knew her sister had dated Nathan. Probably shouldn't matter since she and Nathan were *so* done when it had happened. But it *did* matter, darn it. She didn't like her big sister making a move on her ex. And one of these days, she and Pam were going to have to talk about that. But for now, she changed the subject. "Speaking of families, how're Jake and Terri doing?"

Now he gave her a *real* smile. "They're great. I know you've kept up with what's going on here in Royal, so I'm guessing you know they have twin boys and a little girl?"

"Yeah," she said, smiling wistfully. "Last time I came home to visit my dad before he—well, I made sure you were nowhere around and I met Terri and the kids in town."

Nodding, he said only, "The twins are in kindergarten now and Emily's talking all the time."

A small ache settled in her chest, thinking about Nathan's nephews and niece. Children always did that to her, though—made her remember that she'd been cheated out of her child. Amanda had been playing what-if for more than seven years—wondering how her life might be different if only she hadn't lost Nathan's child. They'd have married, of course—Nathan wouldn't have had it any other way. But would they be happy? Or would he have always felt trapped by circumstances? Would she always wonder if he really loved her or had married her solely out of duty? Questions she would never have the answers to.

She tried to shake them off. "Emily's almost two now, isn't she?"

"Yeah, and a beauty. Has Jake wrapped around her tiny fingers, too." He chuckled and shook his head. "Hard to believe sometimes that Jake's a father, but he's damn good at it."

*So would you have been,* she couldn't help thinking. And maybe his thoughts were mirroring hers because his features slid into more somber lines.

A few miles of silence filled the big black car before Nathan took a turn she recognized.

"So we're not going to the ranch house at all."

"Nope."

"We're going to the river."

"That's the plan."

Nerves jittered and Amanda told herself not to build anything out of this. After all, Nathan had grown up on this land. He and Jake had spent most of their childhoods at the river, fishing, swimming, avoiding chores. For him, this place was just a part of his life. There was no reason to believe that Nathan felt the same…affection for this spot that she did. For Amanda, this river was magical. This one slice of his family's ranch would always be special to her.

Cutting right through the heart of the Battlelands, the fast-moving river was shaded on either bank by ancient live oaks. It was cool and green and lush. As they approached, she couldn't help remembering—and didn't try too hard to stop—that she and Nathan had been in this private place when they made love for the first time so long ago.

Her heartbeat quickened as the memories inside her mind played out like a movie. She could see them both so easily. Young, eager, and for her at least, so much in love she was drowning in the overflow of emotions. Nerves had been thick, but desire was more prominent. It was as if in this one place, time had stopped. The world had dropped away and she became a part of the one man she had always wanted.

Was he remembering? Did he think about that night and all the nights that had followed? Did he have the same regrets she did? Or had he really moved on from their shared past—and if he had, why were they here together now?

The sun was so low now, that only the barest hint of color remained in the sky. Amanda turned her head to the side, looking away from Nathan. What was she supposed to think about this? What was he expecting? Was he deliberately trying to recreate that night? Did he really think that after all these years, all it would take is this one romantic setting and time would roll back?

Oh, God. What if he was right?

The Texas landscape stretched out for miles beneath a faintly rose-colored sky. Grasses waved in a sultry wind on either side of the lonely road and Amanda drew an uneasy breath. Years without Nathan and now, in a single day, he was wiping away the emptiness and drawing her back into a net designed to reawaken emotions she'd thought long buried. How could he take her from fury to desire so easily? And how could she defend her heart against him when all she really wanted was what they'd once had?

"Look familiar?" he asked, voice deep enough to rumble along her spine like tentative fingertips.

"Really does," she said, steeling herself before she turned to look at his profile in the growing darkness. She couldn't read on his face what he was thinking. As always, he had tucked his emotions away, offering the world no peek at what he was feeling. “Why are we here, Nathan?”

He glanced at her, then shifted his gaze back to the road. “We need to talk and I couldn’t think of a more private place.”

Oh, it was private all right, Amanda thought as another slow swirl of anticipation spread through her. This could be dangerous, she warned herself, but at the same time, she wasn’t that young, desperately-in-love girl anymore. She’d grown and changed and lived through a heartbreak she had thought at the time would kill her. She was strong enough now to withstand the churning emotions inside. Strong enough to hold her own against a man who was an overwhelming presence in her life.

At least, she hoped she was.

Otherwise, history would repeat itself tonight—and she honestly couldn’t have said which she was hoping for.

He pulled the car off the road and steered it toward a stand of oaks. She took a breath and let it out slowly, determined to keep what she was feeling to herself. Shouldn’t be hard since her feelings right now were so jumbled even she was confused.

He parked the truck beside the trees, then gave her a look she couldn't interpret. "Everything should be ready. Let's go."

She had no idea what he was talking about but there was only one way to answer her questions. Besides, Amanda wasn't about to let him know that being here made her feel as if she were off balance on a high wire. She opened the door and stepped out into the warm embrace of the summer air. Tipping her head back, she glanced up at the sky. The first stars were just blinking in and out of existence as clouds scudded past. The wind was soft, like a warm caress, as she walked around the front of the car to join Nathan. "What're you up to?"

He smiled. "Come with me and see."

He held out one hand toward her and Amanda hesitated only a moment before laying her palm against his. She was in this far, she told herself, no point in trying to back out now. Besides, she was curious.

Why had he brought her here? What was

*ready?* And who was this man, anyway? Less than a week ago, he'd told her flat out that he wanted her to leave town. Tonight, he was being Prince Charming. Tall, dark, gorgeous and using his smile like a well-honed weapon.

She was completely unsteady and she thought that was exactly the way he wanted her.

Nathan gave her hand a gentle squeeze, then led her through the trees to the river. The whisper of leaves sounded overly loud, like hushed conversations you couldn't quite make out, and the muted roar of the river grew louder as they walked closer. Wind plucked at her hair, her heels wobbled on the sunbaked ground. Nathan lifted branches out of their way as they passed and she felt herself slipping further and further into the past as memories became as thick as the shadows.

They stepped free of the trees and Amanda stopped dead, pulling her hand free of Nathan's to stare at what lay in front of her. A blue-and-white quilt was spread out on the grass. A hurricane lamp was lit, the flame flickering in the soft breeze. A cooler sat at one side of the blanket and two place settings of china and crystal were laid out, just waiting for them.

It had been different in the past, she thought, mind racing as the years rolled back and suddenly she was a shy, nervous high school senior again. Nathan was home from college and he'd brought her here, to "their spot." He had talked about school, what he was doing, who he was meeting, and all she could do was look at him, storing up image after image in her mind so that when he left again, she wouldn't feel so alone.

They'd had a picnic, right here. Nathan had positioned his car so that the headlights shone down on them and the car radio had provided music. They'd talked and laughed and made plans for a misty future neither of them could fully imagine.

And then they'd made love, right here, beneath the stars, for the first time. Everything had changed for them that night. She could still remember his face, as he rose over her, as she took him inside her. The surge of love, of need, filled her now as it had then and had her turning to look at the man beside her.

"What are you doing, Nathan?"

"Remembering," he said, his gaze fixed on the scene laid out in front of them. Then he turned those eyes on her. "Since you've been back I've been doing a lot of that."

"Me, too."

"And you remember what happened here?"

"Not likely to forget," she said with a lightness she didn't feel.

"Good," he said and took her hand again, drawing her toward the scene so meticulously laid out.

It really didn't matter, but she heard herself ask, "Who did all of this?"

"Louisa," he told her just before he eased down to the quilt and drew her down beside him. "She probably had Henry drive her out here and help, but she packed the cooler and set everything up."

Louisa Diaz, the housekeeper at Battlelands. She'd been running that ranch house for twenty years. Of course Nathan would go to her for help. "Wasn't she curious about why you wanted this set up?"

"If she was, she'd never admit it," he said, opening the cooler to draw out a bottle of chilled white wine. He poured two glasses and handed her one.

"We've got strawberries and whipped cream and some of Louisa's famous pecan cookies, too."

She stared at the golden liquid in her glass. She was still off-kilter. He'd gone to so much trouble, setting all of this up, it made her wonder what was behind it all. Just memories? Or was there something more? "It seems you've thought of everything."

"I think so."

"The question remains," she said. "Why?"

He sighed heavily, impatiently. And suddenly he seemed more like the Nathan she'd been dealing with since returning to Royal rather than the younger man she'd given her heart to.

"Does there have to be a reason? Can't we just enjoy it?"

Enjoy it. Reliving a memory that was so cherished it still haunted her dreams? Remember a time when she'd had the world at her fingertips—only to lose it a year later? Pain floated just beneath the surface and Amanda had to fight it back. If she knew what he wanted, expected, maybe this would be easier. But because she couldn't read him, she was left to stumble around in the dark. She took a sip of wine, letting the dry, icy flavor ease the tightness in her throat.

Silence blossomed between them and seemed to grow unchecked for what felt like an eternity before Nathan spoke, shattering the stillness.

"There's no great plan here, Amanda." His voice was deep, and each word seemed to rumble along her spine. "I just wanted to bring you to a place where we could talk."

"And you chose *here*."

A flicker of a smile touched his mouth then faded almost instantly. "You're not the only one who remembers, you know. This was a good spot for us, once."

"Yes," she agreed, her own voice sounding strained and rough. "It was. But Nathan—"

He shook his head. "But nothing. We're here. We'll talk. Have dessert. Relax, Amanda."

Relax?

This from the most tightly wound man she'd ever known?

She looked into his brown eyes and tried to see beyond what he was showing her. But he'd clearly gotten more adept over the years at hiding what he was thinking, feeling, and Amanda was left to take him at his word. Dangerous? Maybe.

But she couldn't ask him to take her home now. She'd look as though she were afraid to be here alone with him and she wouldn't give him that much power. Besides, she could consider this a test of her own resolve. If she and Nathan were going to live here in Royal together, then she had to get past the desire that swept through her every time he was near. She could hardly live her life in a constant state of expectation.

"Okay," she said at last, taking another sip of her wine. "We'll talk."

He gave her a quick, disarming grin that jolted her heartbeat into a thundering gallop and she knew that for her, at least, there wouldn't be any *relaxing* happening tonight.

"I came better prepared this time, too," he said and reached behind the cooler for a small, battery-operated radio. He turned it on and a woman's voice soared into the shadows, singing of love. "Remember the battery on my old truck died that night? Left the radio playing too long and we had to use the ranch walkie-talkie to get Henry to come out and give us a jump?"

She remembered. She also remembered the knowing look Henry had given the two of them. But the ranch foreman hadn't said a word. He'd only gotten Nathan's truck running again and then left.

"That was embarrassing," she said with a sad smile.

"It was," he agreed, then gave her another quick grin. "But it was worth it."

Her hand tightened on the slender base of the crystal wineglass. Nathan was pushing past all of her defenses, one smile at a time.

She turned away from him and looked out over the river. At its widest point, it was no more than six feet across, but it was a wild river, fed from the distant mountains and left unchecked. The water frothed on the surface, slapping against the banks and over rocks worn smooth over time. While she watched, a trout jumped from the water only to splash back down. Wind sighed through the trees, rattling the leaves.

It was perfect.

A summer night, with the stars overhead. Soft music playing accompaniment to the roar of the river and the man who had been the great love of her life at her side. How many times had she wished for just this over the years?

She looked at Nathan as he reached into the cooler and pulled out two cookies. Handing one to her, he smiled and said, "You always did like Louisa's pecan cookies."

Her heart fisted in her chest. He looked so damn…harmless. And he so wasn't.

"You're evil," she said, nipping the cookie from his fingers and taking a bite.

He nodded. "You used to like that about me."

"There are a lot of things I used to like."

"But not anymore." The words were clipped. Cool.

"I didn't say that."

"Didn't have to," he told her and then shrugged as he took a bite of his cookie. "I feel the same way."

"Good to know," she muttered, as her foolishly hopeful heart sunk a little in her chest.

"Things've changed," he said.

"If that's what you brought me out here to tell me," Amanda said, "you wasted your time. I already knew that."

"But the thing is," he said, as if she hadn't spoken at all, "*some* things don't change."

He reached out and stroked the tip of his fingers down the back of her hand and along her arm. Amanda shivered.

"Not fair." She pulled her hand free of him and dropped the cookie to the quilt before she stood up and moved to the edge of the river.

Music continued to sail into the deepening night. The river rushed on and, above her, the stars were glittering against the dark sky.

She heard him stand, then walk up behind her. When his hands dropped onto her shoulders, she was already braced for the heat that poured from his body into hers.

"Why the hell should I play fair?" he demanded and turned her around to face him.

"Why are you playing at all?" she countered and waited, watching his features in the indistinct light.

"Because I can't get you out of my head," he

admitted, his voice harsh and deep, as if it were crawling up from the center of him.

If he could admit at least that much, then she could, too. “I feel the same way.”

He slid his hands up and down her upper arms as if chasing away a chill she didn’t have. In fact, she was so hot at the moment, she couldn’t imagine *ever* being cold again.

Amanda took a breath, tipped her head back to look up at him and said, “Wine. Cookies. Music.” She waved one hand at the frothy river beside them. “This place. What is it you want, Nathan? Truth.”

“Truth.” He tasted the word as if trying to decide if he liked the idea of it or not. Finally, though, he nodded and said, “Truth is, Amanda, there’s a lot of history between us and until we get it sorted out, life in Royal’s going to be harder than it has to be for both of us.”

Disappointment flashed through her before she could stop it. Of course that’s why he’d done all this. To soften her up. To make her malleable enough to agree to however he wanted to handle things. So much for change, she thought glumly.

"We've already had our 'talk,' Nathan."

"Yeah, we did," he agreed. "But it wasn't enough."

She pulled away from him and walked even closer to the river's edge, where spray reached up from the water's surface to kiss her skin. She turned her face up to the sky and fixed her gaze on one star in particular. It was a focus point, to center her thoughts, to gather her frazzled nerves.

She didn't want to talk about the past anymore. It only brought pain. Still watching that star, she asked, "What more is there to say, Nathan?"

She heard him move to stand behind her again. She felt the heat of his body reaching out for hers. Felt the frisson of something incredible that she *always* felt when close to Nathan.

Once again, his hands came down on her shoulders and a whip of electricity snaked through her in an instant. She closed her eyes and took a breath to steady herself—an idea that went to hell the moment he started speaking. "Can we leave the past where it is, Amanda? Live here in town without going back there?"

"I want to," she said and it was the truth. The

past was pain and she'd had enough of that to last a lifetime.

"Then we make a pact. We deal with the present. Starting fresh."

"Just like that?" Was it even possible? she asked herself.

"Won't be easy," he admitted, "but it's easier than hauling the past around with us wherever we go."

It sounded good, but she wasn't as sure as he was that it could be done. But, talking with him, being with him, without the hurtful memories, was worth taking the chance.

"A pact," she agreed and held out one hand.

He looked at it, smiled, then took her hand in his, smoothing his fingers over her knuckles. His voice was soft, low and as mesmerizing as the rush of the river below.

"You're still in my blood, Amanda."

Her heart jumped into high gear and she swayed on her feet. But his hands only tightened on her shoulders. He bent his head until his mouth was beside her ear. His voice came again and his warm breath dusted her skin.

"I think about you. Dream about you. *Want* you."

"Nathan…" Her blood felt as if it were bubbling in her veins.

He spun her around, pulled her close and took her right hand in his left. Confused, Amanda only stared at him, until he said, "Dance with me."

He didn't give her a chance to answer. To decide yes or no. Instead, he began to sway to the music and she let herself move with him. He held her tightly, her body pressed along the length of his and she felt…everything, just as he'd wanted her to.

Her body lit up inside as desire pulsed like a beacon deep within her. He must have sensed it. Must have felt her body's surrender because he dipped his head to steal a hard, fast kiss that left her reeling.

"Tell me you don't the feel the same damn thing," he demanded.

Amanda knew that if she looked into his eyes again, the very foundation of what little self-control she'd managed to cling to would be shaken.

But she couldn't resist. Couldn't deprive herself of the chance to see those dark brown eyes flashing with need again.

The moment she did, she felt herself falling into a whirlwind of emotion. Long-buried feelings resurfaced with a vengeance and were tangled up with something new. Something still fragile, but so much deeper than anything she'd known before.

Their dance ended abruptly. He shifted his grip on her, sliding his hands up to cup her face. His thumbs traced the edges of her cheekbones and his gaze moved over her features hungrily. She felt every nerve in her body leap to attention. Every square inch of her wanted him so desperately she trembled with the need.

It would be so easy to give in, she thought wildly as she lost herself in the dark chocolate of his eyes. To surrender to her body's demands. To push away the past and think only of the now. But where would that put them? Where would they go from here?

"Nathan, this is crazy…."

"Nothing wrong with crazy," he murmured and

leaned in to leave a light-as-a-feather kiss on her forehead.

She swallowed hard. “But if we do this—it will only make living in this town together harder.”

He snorted a laugh. “I can’t get much harder.”

“Oh, God.” Her breath caught in her lungs as he pulled her in close to him. Close enough to discover that he was right. Much harder and he’d turn to stone.

A burn started low and deep within her, spreading with a swiftness that made her feel as if she had a sudden fever. A fever only Nathan could assuage.

Shaking her head both at her own thoughts and at him, she pulled free and took a staggering step backward just for an extra measure of safety. Not that she was afraid of Nathan. No, she was more afraid that her good intentions would be blown out of the water by her own need.

“Damn it, Amanda,” he said roughly. “You want this, too. I can feel it.”

“Yes,” she admitted when she could talk around the knot lodged in her throat. “I do. But I’m not going to do it.”

"Why the hell not?"

"Because it wouldn't solve anything, Nathan."

He threw both hands high and wide then let them fall to his sides again. "Why the hell does it have to *solve* anything? We're not kids anymore. Can't it just be what it is and leave it at that?"

"Not between us," she said, a little steadier now that he wasn't touching her. "It's never simple between us, Nathan, and you know it."

He shoved both hands into his jeans pockets and let his head fall back briefly as if looking for patience in the wide Texas sky above them. When he looked at her again, he said, "You can't let go of the past, can you?"

Bristling a little, she countered, "Can you?"

Shaking his head, he pulled one hand free of his pocket and ran it over his face. "Not entirely, no."

"Then how can us sleeping together help?"

"How can it hurt?" he argued.

"Nathan, sex doesn't solve a problem, it only creates *new* problems."

"Maybe that's enough for now," he said tightly.

"Not for me," she answered.

"What the hell do you want, then?"

A thousand disjointed thoughts swept through her mind in one confusing instant. What did she want? *Him,* mostly. She'd tried to fool herself into believing that she just wanted to move on. To find a new man and build a life with him.

But there were no other men for Amanda. There was only Nathan, now and always. She wanted what they hadn't had before. Trust. Love. A future. And she knew Nathan wasn't interested in anything like that.

So that left her exactly where?

Alone, she thought. She'd be alone.

He closed the gap between them in one long stride and grabbed her up close again. Here was the danger, she thought. Feeling him pressed close to her, knowing that he wanted her as much as she wanted him. But want wasn't enough, as they'd already discovered.

"Don't make this harder," she whispered.

"Why should I make it easy?" he asked.

She looked up at him and when he kissed her, Amanda lost herself in him. His mouth covered hers with a fierce tenderness that quickly became a dance of desperation. Their tongues met again and again, stroking, caressing, tasting. Hunger built and spread, wrapping them both in a wash of heat that was inescapable. His hands swept up and down her back and finally came to rest on her behind. He held her tightly to him and ground his hips into hers. She gasped and lifted one leg instinctively, wrapping it around his thigh, trying, but failing to bring him even closer.

His mouth continued to overwhelm her and all of Amanda's good intentions were swept away on a tide of passion too staggering to fight. Her mind splintered under the onslaught of too many sensations. It had been so long, was her only coherent thought. So long since she'd felt his hands on her body, his breath on her face. How could she not have him? What did it matter what happened tomorrow, if tonight, she could have *this?*

One of his strong hands held her thigh up along his hip, his fingers digging into her flesh. With his free hand, he lifted the hem of her skirt, then slipped his hand beneath the hem of her panties and down to the trembling, heated core of her.

At the first brush of his fingers, Amanda

gasped, and tore her mouth from his. Reeling, she tipped her head back and stared into his eyes as he stroked her hot, damp center. His brown eyes were flashing with fire and need. His breath came as fast and sharp as hers. Her fingers clutched at his shoulders, as she fought for balance and for the orgasm that was rushing toward her.

He dipped one finger and then two into her depths, stroking both inside and out as he plunged and withdrew in a rapid rhythm that tortured as it pleasured. Amanda's hips rocked into his hand as she struggled to find the release that he was promising her. Her mind was shutting down. Who needed to think when he was offering her so much to *feel?*

Again and again, she whimpered and twisted against his touch. His thumb rolled over one sensitive spot and she cried out his name in a broken voice torn from a throat nearly too tight to allow breath.

"Come for me," he whispered, kissing her mouth, her eyes, her nose. "Come now, Amanda, and let me see you shatter."

Stars shone overhead. A Texas wind caressed

her bare skin. Her lover's eyes held hers. And Amanda surrendered to the inevitable with a groan of release and a whispered sigh that was his name.

# Seven

She was limp in his grasp and Nathan had never felt more alive. His body hard and aching, his pulse scrambling, he continued to stroke her intimately, loving the feel of her slick flesh beneath his fingers. Her breath hitched and she jerked in his arms as her still-sensitive body reacted to his touch.

No woman in the world affected him like this one did. With just a sigh, she could inflame him or bring him to his knees. Which is why he was here, he reminded himself. This was the plan. To have sex with her again so that he could walk away. He looked down into her face and saw a soft, satisfied smile. Saw her meadow-green eyes glazed with passion. Saw the rapid pulse beat at the base of her throat and he wasn't thinking about walking away. He was thinking only of burying himself inside her. Feeling her body close around his again.

"Nathan…that was…"

"Foreplay," he groaned past the hard knot of need lodged in his throat and waited for her reaction. He touched her again and she trembled. In his arms, she felt vulnerable, soft, and every protective instinct he had roared to life. In that moment, he wanted to stand between her and the rest of the world. He wanted to always see her like this, looking up at him with stars in her eyes and a breathless plea on her lips.

Seconds ticked past as she looked into his eyes. He held perfectly still. He wouldn't touch her again until she said yes. Until she admitted that sex was the *one* thing they both could agree on. That they both needed. He hoped to hell she'd say it. If she still said no, it just might kill him.

She lifted one hand to cup his cheek and stroked her thumb along his cheekbone. "I'm tired of being sensible," she said. "I don't want to think about tomorrow. I only want tonight. With you."

He waited a beat or two, letting her words sink in. Then, for his own sanity, he demanded, "You're sure?"

She smiled and linked her arms behind his neck. "About this, yes."

"Thank God," he muttered and spun her around in a quick circle before lowering her to the quilt spread beneath the gnarled, twisted arms of the oaks surrounding them.

Quickly, they worked to clear the quilt, setting the wine aside and shifting the cooler off into the thick grass. The radio played on, music shifting now to a low, throbbing beat that seemed to echo what each of them was feeling.

They turned to each other, tearing at clothing, needing to touch only skin. Needing to feel the heat that flesh against flesh created. The summer wind slid over them as hands and mouths rediscovered the magic that pulsed between them.

Nathan couldn't seem to touch her enough. The feel of her soft, smooth skin beneath his fingers fed the fire inside that was engulfing him. His brain hazed out, his vision narrowed until all he saw was *her.* The woman who had haunted him for years. The woman he'd lost and never forgotten.

He eased back, taking a moment to just look at her, enjoy this moment when she was his again. Her hair spilled across the quilt beneath her. Her long, tanned limbs were lean and smooth and her breasts were high and full. His hands itched to cup them, to tease those pebbled nipples until she was moaning and arching into his touch.

Shaking his head, he murmured, "Been thinking about this since that first day I saw you in the diner."

She laughed a little and the sound rose over the roar of the river to become part of the music of the night. "You mean when you walked in all fiery-eyed, wanting me to leave town?"

"Yeah, only I didn't want you out of town as much as I just *wanted* you," Nathan told her, dipping his head to taste first one dark nipple and then the other.

She gasped, then sighed, a slow exhalation of breath that seemed to slide right into the heart of him. When he lifted his head again, she looked up into his eyes and said, "You hid it really well, being all crabby."

He gave her a quick grin. "Couldn't let the town gossips know what I was thinking. Hell, I didn't want *you* to know what I was thinking."

"Oh, me neither," she admitted, holding his head to her breast. Her fingers threaded through his short hair, her nails dragging across his scalp.

He was on fire. His whole damn body felt as if it were lit up from the flames about to swallow him. "Shoulda done this days ago."

"Oh, yeah," she whispered and arched into him as he moved down her body, trailing damp kisses along her skin…down her chest, along the line of her stomach and across her abdomen. She tasted of summer and smelled like a spring meadow. He was surrounded by her taste, scent, touch. And still it wasn't enough. His body ached like a bad tooth. He needed her and damned if he wanted to *need.* Being sucked into a maelstrom of emotions hadn't been the plan. The plan was simply to bed her, so he could get her out of his system once and for all.

*The plan.* He fought to hold on to it. To remember why it was important. Nathan Battle didn't do anything without a damn plan and once it was made, it was golden.

And yet…his brain shied away from thinking at all. Nathan wanted to concentrate solely on this moment, not what had led to it or what might come after. All he wanted right now was to revel in finally having her here, beneath his hands again.

Her body was long and slim with just the right amount of curves to tempt a man. In the starlight, her skin seemed like warm honey. He dragged the tips of his fingers across her flat belly and smiled to himself when she sucked in a gulp of air. He traced the tan lines that striped over her breasts and then along the narrow strip of paler skin that lay across the triangle of light brown curls at the juncture of her thighs.

"You wear a tiny bikini," he murmured and wished he'd seen her in it.

She smiled. "No point in wearing a big one, is there?"

"Nope, guess not," he agreed, sliding one hand down to cup her heat. "What color is it?"

She gasped and rocked her hips into his hand. "What? Color? What?"

"Your bikini, Amanda," he whispered, "what color is it?"

He dipped a finger into her heat and she hissed a breath. "Is that really important right now?"

"Humor me," he told her and swirled the tip of his finger around an already sensitive spot.

"Okay, okay, just don't stop," she ordered, then swallowed hard. "It's white. With red..." She broke off and shuddered, as he continued to stroke her with slow deliberation.

"Red what?"

"Huh? Red? Right." She nodded, licked her lips and wiggled her hips into his touch. "Red, um, dots. Polka dots."

"Sounds nice."

"Uh-huh," she whispered. "I'll be sure to show you sometime. But for right now could we..."

"You want more?" he asked, knowing she did, drawing out the suspense, the waiting, the wanting, for both of them.

"I want it all." Her eyes snapped open and she met his gaze squarely. "Honestly, Nathan, if you don't get inside me within the next minute or so…"

"You'll what?" He grinned at her, enjoying the frustration in her eyes, in her voice. "Leave?"

She blew out a breath and scowled at him. "Funny. No, I'm not leaving, but Nathan—"

He rose up over her, looked down into her eyes and whispered, "You're still so beautiful."

"I'm glad you think so." She sighed and reached for him, but he pulled back, grabbed the jeans he'd tossed aside a few minutes before and rummaged in the pockets until he came up with a foil square.

"Pretty sure of yourself, weren't you?" she asked wryly.

"Pretty sure of *us,*" he told her as he ripped the foil open, then took another moment to sheathe himself.

Her expression was carefully blank as his gaze met hers and she asked, "Is there an us, Nathan?"

That was a good question, he thought, his eyes locked on hers. And he didn't have an answer.

Yesterday, he might have flatly said no. Tomorrow, he might do the same. But now… "There is tonight."

A flicker of sorrow danced across her eyes and was gone again so quickly he could almost convince himself he hadn't noticed it at all. He didn't want to hurt her, but damned if he'd pretend something that wasn't so. Besides, he didn't want to think beyond the moment. *Us?* No, there was no us. But there was *now.*

"No more thinking," he murmured and ended any further conversation by taking her mouth in a kiss that left them both breathless. His brain went blank and his body took over. Her hands slid up and down his back, her neat nails scraping across his skin, letting him know that the hunger that crouched inside him lived within her, too.

The past dropped away as they found each other again in the most elemental way. Every touch was a reaffirmation of what they'd once been. Every kiss and gasped breath was a celebration of what they were discovering now. In the warm summer air, they gave and took from each other until passion was a living, breathing entity, wrapping them so tightly together they might never completely be apart again.

They rolled across the quilt, arms and legs wrapped around each other as the river rushed on and the music continued to pump into the night air. Wind whispered through the trees and their strained breathing added to the symphony.

His hands moved over her body and every touch was achingly familiar while, at the same time, it all felt new, electrifying. As if this were their first time coming together.

He pushed her over onto her back and went up on one elbow to look down at her. She looked like a summer goddess, stretched out on that blue-and-white quilt, with starlight dancing on her skin. His breath caught when she licked her lips and smiled up at him. Her eyes were glazed with a burning desire that reached out to engulf him in the same flames. The fire felt good after so many years in the cold, he thought wildly. But he wasn't about to wait another damn minute before claiming her and all she was.

He shifted, kneeling between her legs and when she parted her thighs and lifted her arms to him in welcome, he groaned in satisfaction. He pushed himself home in one long, smooth stroke and hissed out a breath at the sensation of her hot, tight body gripping his.

She gasped, lifted her legs and locked them around his hips, pulling him deeper, tighter. She arched, her hips rising to meet his, drawing him as close as she could. Then she trembled as pleasure whipped through her—a bright, white-hot thing that glittered in her eyes. He felt her pleasure with her every sigh. Felt the tension coiling in her body just from the way she moved with him.

As if they were somehow connected on a deeper level than just physically, he felt what she did, knew when he looked into her eyes how close she was to climax. He knew her as he'd known no other woman. Her body was as familiar to him as his own. Her passion as important as his own.

Her hands clutched at his back, his shoulders, his arms. Every strangled breath and sigh fed the fires inside him. His hips pistoned into hers as he withdrew from her body only to plunge deep inside her heat again.

Her gasps and sighs filled him, pushing him harder, faster, as he quickened the rhythm between them and she rushed to meet him. He took her mouth, his kiss demanding, hungry. She had demands, too. Silent, desperate demands that he met eagerly.

"Nathan. Nathan." His name became a chant that was caught up by the wind and tossed into the night sky. She whispered and pleaded, moving her body into his, fighting for the release that waited for her.

And when the first tremor hit, she clung to him, riding out wave after wave of pleasure tearing through her. Nathan felt her body fist on his as her completion took her. Only then did he give himself up to the coiled tension inside, finally releasing his stranglehold on control, surrendering to what only Amanda could do to him.

His body exploded, his mind shattered and when he collapsed against her, Amanda's arms came around him in the darkness.

Amanda's heartbeat was racing. With Nathan's heavy weight covering her, she felt, for the first time in years, *complete.* Ridiculous to admit, even to herself, but without him in her life she'd always felt as though something was missing. Something vital.

Now, here it was.

But she didn't know how long this could last.

He'd already told her that as far as he was concerned they weren't together. This was just sex. *Stupendous* sex, but just sex. If she made more of it than that, she would be setting herself up for pain and disappointment.

He shifted and rolled to one side of her, drawing her with him until she was nestled against his chest. Amanda listened to the sound of his rapid heartbeat and knew that he was as affected as she was. Some consolation in that, she supposed.

The silence between them stretched on for what seemed forever until she simply couldn't stand it anymore. Best, she told herself, to be the one to speak first. To set a tone that would let him know that she wasn't going to swoon into his arms or cry and beg him to stay.

Not that she didn't want to, but he didn't have to know that, did he?

"Nathan, that was—"

"Yeah," he agreed. "It was."

"So," she said, lifting her head to look at him, "come here often?"

He grinned, fast and sharp and her breath caught.

"Haven't been here in years," he said. "Not since—"

He stopped, but now she knew that he hadn't brought another woman to what was most definitely "their" place. Funny how much comfort that brought her. Oh, he was no monk and during the time they were apart—there had no doubt been *dozens* of women in his life. She winced at that thought. But at least he hadn't brought them here.

"It's beautiful here," she told him, glancing at the moonlight on the water.

"Yeah, it is. Look, Amanda…"

Oh, that sounded like the beginnings of a we-have-to-talk speech. Which she really didn't want to hear at the moment. She preferred the teasing, tempting Nathan who had just shattered her so completely. She didn't want to talk to the dutiful and honorable Nathan. Not now.

So she just wouldn't give him the opportunity to turn this moment into a regret-filled this-will-never-happen-again speech. Abruptly, she sat up and reached for her shirt. Dragging it on over her head, she flipped her hair back over her shoulder and asked, "How about some of that wine?"

He studied her for a long minute, then sat up and reached for his own clothes. "Sure, that'd be good."

"And cookies," she reminded him, determined to keep a cheerful, nonchalant attitude. Standing up, she stepped into her panties and then her skirt, smoothing the material before sitting down on the quilt again. "I think we need more cookies."

Once he was dressed, he sat down opposite her on the quilt and watched her warily, as if she were a time bomb with a faulty fuse and could go off any second. "Cookies."

"Why not?" she asked. "Don't you remember? Sex always gives me an appetite."

Unexpectedly, he smiled as he poured them

each a fresh glass of wine. "I do remember all of the picnics we had in bed."

Stillness washed over her as memories slammed into her mind. So many nights they'd spent in bed, laughing, loving and then feeding each other whatever they'd been able to find in the refrigerator. "We had a lot of good times, Nathan."

He handed her a full glass, then clinked his to hers. "Yeah, we did. But, Amanda…"

She cut him off and saw his jaw tighten at being interrupted. "Let's just leave it there, okay? We had good times back then and we had a good time tonight. Isn't that what you said earlier? We have tonight?"

"Yeah, I did."

"So, let's enjoy it."

"You are the most confusing woman I've ever known."

Amanda laughed. "I think I'm flattered."

"You would be," he said wryly. "You always knew how to twist me around until I didn't know which end was up."

He sounded almost wistful and Amanda's heart lurched in her chest. Memories were swimming in the air between them, rising and falling as swiftly as the frothy waves on the nearby river. Amanda took a sip of her wine to ease the knot in her throat before she trusted herself to speak. "You used to like that about me."

"Yeah," he admitted. "I did."

Her gaze caught with his. "I've missed you, Nathan."

"I've missed you, too."

And maybe, Amanda told herself, for tonight, that was enough.

"You had sex."

"Piper!" Amanda jolted and looked around the diner guiltily, making sure no one was within earshot. Thankfully, most of the lunch crowd was long gone and she and her friend had the back of the diner practically to themselves. Amanda grabbed her cup of coffee for a sip, then asked, "Could you say that any louder?"

"Probably," Piper said. "Want me to try?"

"No!" Amanda shook her head and tried for a little dignity. What? Was the truth stenciled on her forehead? *I had sex with Nathan last night.* Who else had noticed? Oh, God.

"I don't know what you're talking about," Amanda told her, deciding to plead ignorance and let it go at that.

"Sure," her old friend said with a smirk. "I'll buy that. And any bridges you might have lying around."

Amanda frowned and leaned back into the rush of cool air pouring down on her from the overhead air-conditioning vent. Irritating to be read so easily—and by someone she hadn't even seen in years. Well, clearly there was no point in pretending with Piper. "Fine. Yes. You're right, Ms. Mind Reader."

Piper laughed and took a bite of the lemon meringue pie Amanda had promised her the day before. "Honey, I don't need to read your mind. It's in your eyes—not to mention the whisker burn on your neck."

She slapped one hand to the right side of her throat. A quick tingle whipped through her as she recalled how it had felt, having Nathan's whiskery cheeks buried in the curve of her neck. Of course that didn't mean she wanted the world noticing what she'd been up to. Amanda had been so sure she'd managed a makeup miracle. Now she didn't know why she had bothered.

"Honestly, I don't know how they can call that foundation 'full coverage,'" she muttered. "I should send them an email, complaining."

"You do that," Piper said with a chuckle. "So, how is Nathan?"

"He's...*good*." Better than good. Fabulous, really. A smile curved her mouth as she remembered the night before.

By the time Amanda had gotten home, she was more tired and more energized than she'd been in years. Every cell in her body had felt as if it had just come to life after long years of sleep. She'd felt almost like Sleeping Beauty, except that Nathan wasn't exactly Prince Charming and she was no damsel in distress waiting to be rescued.

No, last night hadn't been the beginning of anything. She wouldn't fool herself into hoping for more when she was pretty sure that Nathan was considering what had happened at the river to be just a good time.

But it had been more. For her, at least. Despite what she had said to Nathan, Amanda wasn't a sex-is-just-sex kind of girl. If sex didn't mean anything, what was the point to it all? No. The only reason she had slept with Nathan was because she still had feelings for him.

"And so," Piper persisted, "this means you're back together?"

"No," Amanda said, shaking her head. "I'm not kidding myself about that. Last night was just… last night." She wasn't going to invent dreams and let them soar only to come crashing back to earth again. She'd already lived through that pain once and really had no desire to do it one more time. "Nathan and I didn't work out before, remember?"

Piper winced. "I know, but you're both different now."

"Are we?" she wondered aloud. Amanda had been doing a lot of thinking about this since the night before. Sure, they were older, hopefully wiser, but was it enough to make a new relationship possible? Did Nathan even want a new relationship with her?

She was getting a headache.

"I don't know," she said finally. "Nathan will always be important to me. But—"

"No buts," Piper insisted. "There don't have to be any buts."

Amanda chuckled. "In a perfect world…"

A loud noise from across the room caught her attention and Amanda glanced at her sister, who was slamming the coffeepot back onto the warming burner. It was a wonder the pot hadn't shattered. Amanda frowned when Pam turned her head long enough to fire a glare at her.

"Wow, Pam's in a good mood today."

"Yeah," Amanda said. "She's been like this all morning."

"Not surprising," Piper told her. "She's been after Nathan for years and she's probably guessed by now that she's never going to get him."

"What?"

"You probably know that she and Nathan went out a couple times while you were gone." When Amanda nodded, Piper continued. "Well, it didn't go anywhere. Nathan wasn't interested. And let's just say if I could notice the whisker burn on your neck, then Pam noticed, too."

"Perfect." So not only was her life in turmoil over Nathan, but she also had to worry about her sister's anger, too.

Piper shot a quick glance at Pam over her shoulder before turning back to Amanda. She leaned in closer to say, "Everybody knows Pam's been crazy about Nathan since school. Just like everyone knows that she's jealous of you."

"Everyone but me," Amanda said and picked up her coffee for a sip. Yes, she knew Pam had had a crush on Nathan when they were in school. What girl *hadn't* back then? But jealous? "Why should she be jealous of me?"

"Hmm…" Piper pretended to ponder the question. "Let's see. You're younger, prettier, you've got a college degree she never bothered to go after and most importantly—you have Nathan."

*"Had."*

Piper's eyebrows lifted. "You sure about the past tense, there?"

The old-fashioned jukebox was playing in the corner, some classic rock and roll song streaming through the one large speaker. A couple of people sat at the counter having a late lunch and two elderly women occupied a booth and shared tea and cake. Most people around here stayed home on Sunday and had family meals together so it was a slow day for the diner, which was both a burden and a blessing.

Since Amanda hadn't gotten much sleep the night before, she was grateful to not be so busy. But not being busy meant that Pam had the time to make Amanda's life miserable. Which, she had to say, her sister was getting really good at.

But the worst part about a slow day at the diner? It gave Amanda too much time to think. Too much time to wonder about what had happened the night before between her and Nathan. And no matter how much thought she put into the situation, she was no closer to understanding it.

She knew that the two of them together were magical. But she also knew that didn't guarantee a happy ending.

"Whatever you're thinking," Piper said quietly, "you should stop it. Doesn't look like it's making you happy."

"It's not." Amanda took a bite of her pie and let the dense lemon flavoring explode on her tongue. When she'd swallowed, she said, "I don't know that last night meant a darn thing, Piper."

"If you want it to mean something, it will."

She laughed shortly. "Not that simple. What if I want it and Nathan doesn't?"

"*Make* him want it," Piper suggested with a shrug.

"Oh, well, that should be easy," she mused.

"No, it won't," Piper told her. "Nothing worth having comes easy. The question is, do you want him?"

"Wish that was the only question," she murmured and finished off her pie.

# Eight

A few days later, Amanda realized she had forgotten just how much she enjoyed small-town Fourth of July celebrations.

All of Royal seemed to be gathered at the park. The sun glared down from a brassy sky and promised to get even hotter as the day wore on. Nobody seemed to mind much. Texans were a tough bunch and no matter how miserable the heat and humidity, they didn't let it get in the way of a good time.

There was a community baseball game in full swing on the diamond. Picnic blankets dotted the grass and families settled in for a long day that wouldn't end until after the big fireworks show. Kids raced through the park, laughing and shouting, oblivious to the heat that was already beginning to wilt their parents.

Dozens of game booths were scattered around the park, each of them offering chances to win everything from goldfish to teddy bears. And at the far end of the parking lot, a small carnival had set up shop and the taped calliope music was fiercely cheerful.

Amanda grinned at the little boy in front of the booth she was manning. He was about six, with a missing front tooth, hair that was too long and a T-shirt already stained with what looked like mustard. At the moment, he was biting his lip and considering the last softball he held. He had already gone through most of his pocket money, buying chances to knock over bowling pins with the softball to win a prize.

"It sure is harder than it looks, ma'am," he said with a shake of his head.

"It is, isn't it?" Amanda was trying to figure out a way she could "help" the boy win, when Nathan walked up.

A now familiar flash of excitement zipped through her at just the sight of him. He wore a beige uniform shirt, with the sheriff star on his chest glittering in the sunlight. His jeans were faded, his boots were scuffed and his hat was pulled low enough on his forehead to throw his eyes into shadow.

It had been a few days since their night by the river and since then, things had been…different between them. Well, of course—they'd had sex. Things would be *different,* not that they'd slept together since. But there was less tension between them. And, she thought wistfully, more confusion.

"Afternoon, Amanda," he said, then shifted his gaze to the boy. "Carter, how you doing?"

"Not so good, Sheriff," the boy answered and scowled at the one softball he had left to throw. "I figured I'd win one of those teddy bears for my baby sister." He shrugged. "Girls like that sort of thing, but like I told Miss Amanda, it's a lot harder than it looks."

"What're you doin' running around on your own? Where're your folks?"

Carter pointed over one shoulder at a young family sitting on a blanket under a tree. "They're all right there."

"That's good." Nathan dropped one hand on the boy's narrow shoulder, then ruffled his hair. "Maybe we can try together, what do you think?"

The boy looked up at him as if Nathan were wearing a cape and had just swooped in to the rescue.

Amanda watched Nathan with the child and swallowed a sigh. If she hadn't lost their baby, it would now be about this boy's age. Boy? Or girl? It had been too early to know at the time, but that hadn't stopped her from wondering. From picturing what her child with Nathan might have been like. And in this boy, with the light brown hair and brown eyes, she saw…what might have been. And the tiny ache that settled in the corner of her heart felt like an old friend.

"How about I give you a hand?" Nathan asked, then flashed a smile at Amanda. "That is, if Miss Amanda doesn't mind."

"That'd be great, Sheriff," Carter answered, then turned to Amanda and asked, "Is it okay?"

"Well, you know, back when the sheriff was in high school, he was the star pitcher."

Nathan smiled at her as if pleased she remembered. How could she forget? She'd spent hours in the bleachers at Royal high school, watching Nathan play ball. And every time he went up to bat, he'd look at her first, as if he were checking she was still there, still watching.

"Really?" Carter brightened up even further.

"No pressure," Nathan muttered with a shake of his head.

"C'mon, Sheriff," she said and stood back as Nathan took the ball from Carter and tossed it in the air a couple times to get its weight. "Show us what you've got."

He nodded at the boy then winked at Amanda. "Well, now, let's see what we can do."

He wound up, threw the ball and sent three bowling pins clattering to the floor. Carter whooped with delight and even Amanda had to applaud.

"You won, Sheriff!" Carter clapped, too. "Nice throw!"

Amanda picked up one of the teddy bears lining the prize shelf and handed it to Nathan, who gave it to Carter.

"My baby sister's gonna like this a lot. Thanks, Sheriff!" Clutching the bear, the boy took off and was swallowed by the crowd moments later.

Amanda looked up at Nathan and smiled in approval. "That was nice of you."

"Carter's a good kid." Nathan shrugged and leaned one hip against the edge of the booth. His gaze swept up and down her body thoroughly until she felt a heat that had nothing to do with a hot Texas day.

"So," he said, "how'd you come to be running the PTA booth?"

"Patti Delfino had to take care of the baby so I offered to help."

"Falling right back into life in Royal, huh?"

"It wasn't that hard," she said. Although being around him *was.* She didn't know where they stood. Didn't know what was going to happen next. They'd had that one incredible night together and since then…nothing. Well, except for him stopping in at the diner a few times a day. But they hadn't been alone again and she was hungering for him. Did he feel the same? Or had he considered that night a one-time thing? A sort of goodbye to the past?

The questions running through her mind were driving her crazy.

A little girl ran up and patted Nathan's thigh to get his attention. When he looked down at her, the girl's big blue eyes fixed on him. "I wanna teddy bear, too."

"You do, huh?" He grinned and looked at Amanda. "Apparently Carter's bragging how he got hold of his bear."

"And what are you going to do about it, Sheriff?" Amanda teased.

He dug in his wallet and slapped down a twenty-dollar bill. "Guess I'll be throwing softballs."

The little girl clapped and bounced up and down in excitement. Amanda handed him three softballs to get him started and then stood back and watched as he mowed through the prize shelf. Over and over again, he threw the balls at the bowling pins and soon he had a crowd of kids surrounding him, each of them waiting to be handed one of the stuffed bears.

Amanda watched him, saw his eyes shining with pleasure, heard him laughing with the children and a part of her wept for what they might have had together. He was so good with kids. He would have been a wonderful father if only…

By the time it was over, the bears were all gone and the last of the children had wandered off, clutching their prizes. When it was just Nathan and Amanda again, he said, "Looks like you're out of business. What do you say we find Patti and hand over the cash box, then you and I go join Jake and Terri for some lunch?"

"Aren't you on duty?"

"I can keep an eye on things—and you—at the same time."

Pleasure whipped through her as she grabbed up the metal cash box and swung her legs over the side of the booth. "I think I'll let you."

He took her hand in his and as they walked through the mob of people, Amanda felt that sense of rightness again. Did he feel it, too?

The rest of the day went by in a sort of blur. It

had been so long since Amanda had really enjoyed a Fourth of July. When she was away, she would sit on the balcony of her apartment and watch distant fireworks alone. She could have gone out with friends, but her heart hadn't been in it. Instead, she had wished to be back here. At home in Royal.

And the town wasn't disappointing her.

After lunch with Jake and Terri and the kids, Nathan and Amanda spent the rest of the day with them. Nathan was called away a few times to settle disputes ranging from an argument over the umpire's call on the baseball field to a broken windshield in the parking lot. He always came back, though, and Amanda saw that with his family, Nathan was more relaxed. More ready to enjoy himself than she remembered him ever being before.

Back in the day, he'd been too driven, too determined to carve out the life he wanted to take the time to slow down with family. Maybe, she thought, they'd both changed enough over the years that they could find a way back to each other.

With the fireworks about to start, Jake and Nathan walked the kids over to get some Sno-Kones, while Amanda and Terri settled on the quilt and waited for the show.

"I'm so glad you're home," Terri said abruptly.

"Oh, me, too. Believe me." Amanda looked around the park at all the familiar faces and smiled to herself. Older couples sat in lawn chairs, holding hands, gazes locked on the sky. Young marrieds herded small children and the older kids raced through the park waving sparklers, flashes of light trailing behind them like high-tech bread crumbs.

Whatever happened between her and Nathan, Amanda was home to stay. "I really did miss this place."

"Hmm," Terri mused. "You missed Royal? Or Nathan?"

"Sadly, both." Terri knew her too well to believe a lie, so why not admit the truth? "But that doesn't mean anything, Terri."

"Sure it does," she said, biting into one of the last pecan cookies with relish. "It means you guys belong together. Everybody knows that."

"Everybody but Nathan," Amanda muttered, glancing at her friend. Terri was tiny, trim and summer cute in a hot pink sundress with spaghetti straps. Her long, dark brown hair was in a single braid that hung down the middle of her back.

As Amanda watched her, Terri licked a crumb from her bottom lip and popped the rest of the cookie into her mouth. As she chewed, she said, "Nathan's been on edge since you got back."

"Great. On edge."

Terri just stared at her for a second, then shook her head. "Seriously? Do you know nothing about men? On edge is just where you want them. That way they're never sure which way to turn."

"And that's a good thing?" Amanda asked with a laugh.

"Absolutely." Terri grabbed a bottle of water and took a long drink. "Why would you want Nathan all relaxed and complacent about you?"

She hadn't thought about it that way, but now she was. Maybe Terri had a point. Kicking off her sandals, Amanda folded her legs under her. Bracing her elbows on her knees, she cupped her chin in her hands and looked at her friend. “So, you keep Jake guessing, do you?”

“All the time, sweetie,” Terri assured her with a laugh. “Why do you think he adores me so?”

“Because he’s smart enough to know how good he’s got it?”

“Well, that, too.” Terri laughed. “But mostly because I keep him on his toes. He’s never sure what I’ll do next.”

As she reached for another cookie, Amanda shook her head. “How do you stay so thin when you eat like this?”

“Won’t be thin for long,” Terri said with a smile and a gentle pat on her belly. “I’m pregnant again.”

Instantly, Amanda felt a quick slice of envy poke at her. Terri had three wonderful kids and a husband who really did adore her. While Amanda was happy for her friend, it was hard not to wish that her own life was as full.

“I saw that,” Terri said and reached out to pat Amanda’s hand. “Sweetie, I’m sorry. I didn’t mean to make you feel badly.”

“Don’t be silly.” Amanda squeezed her hand

and shook her head. "I'm happy for you. Really. I just…" She looked out over the park again, toward the booth where Jake and Nathan shepherded twin five-year-old boys and a darling two-year-old girl. As she watched, Nathan scooped up little Emily and cradled her in one arm. The girl laid her head on Nathan's chest and snuggled in. Smiling sadly, she looked at Terri and admitted, "Sometimes I just wish things were different."

Terri sighed. "Sweetie, maybe it's time to stop wishing and start *making* things different."

Amanda looked back at Nathan in time to see him laugh at something one of the twins said. A jolt of longing hit her hard. That smile of his would always turn her to butter.

Maybe Terri was right, she thought. Maybe it was time to take a stand. To fight for what she wanted. And what she wanted was Nathan.

When the fireworks started, Nathan settled down beside her and Amanda leaned her head back against his broad chest. They stared up at the sky, which was exploding with sound and color. He wrapped one arm around her and held her close and, despite the fact that they were surrounded by people, Amanda felt as if they were the only two people in the world.

The next morning, Amanda woke up to Nathan's kiss at the back of her neck. She smiled lazily, remembering the long night before. After the fireworks, they'd come back to her apartment over the diner and created a few fireworks of their own.

"Good morning."

"Mmm," he murmured, dragging one hand down her side, following the dip of her waist and the curve of her hip. "It's looking pretty good right now."

She smiled, then sighed as his hand moved to slide across her behind. Somehow, they'd crossed a bridge yesterday. Maybe it was the hours spent with his family. Maybe it was just that enough time had passed for them both to realize that they wanted to be together. Whatever the reason, Nathan had stayed here with her last night, not caring that the town gossips would surely notice his car parked in front of her place all night.

When he shifted his hand to cup her breast, Amanda hissed in a breath and rolled onto her back so she could look up at him. She didn't think she'd ever tire of that. His dark eyes could flash with temper, shine with kindness or, like right now, glitter with desire. She lifted one hand to his cheek and scrubbed at his whiskers with her thumb.

Smiling, she whispered, "I'm glad you stayed last night."

"Me, too," he told her and gave her a long, slow, deep kiss that quickened the still-burning embers inside her. "And I'd really like to stay now, but I've gotta get to work."

She glanced at the window, where the soft, early-morning light was sifting through the curtains. "Me, too."

He kissed her again and tenderness welled up between them, stinging Amanda's eyes and tearing at her heart. This is what she wanted. Nathan, all of Nathan. Not just the fire that quickened her blood and made her heart race—but the warmth that touched her soul and made her yearn.

When he lifted his head and looked down into her eyes, he whispered, "Maybe I don't have to leave right this minute."

She nodded and cupped his face in her hands. "I think I could spare some time, too."

And this time when he kissed her, she forgot about everything else and let herself slide into a sensual haze that only he could create.

"Did you hear that?" Pam stopped in front of JT and automatically refilled his coffee cup.

"Hear what?"

"Hannah Poole was telling Bebe Stryker about Nathan's car being out front of the diner all night."

JT sighed, shook his head and took a sip of coffee. "What do you care about that?"

She looked at him as if he'd just grown another head. "The whole town's talking about Nathan and Amanda. If it gets bad enough, he'll leave again."

"Not a chance," JT muttered but Pam hardly heard him.

"I can't believe Amanda's starting up with him again." Huffing out a breath, she added, "I can't believe Nathan would *want* her again. After what she did…"

JT's eyes narrowed. "Thought you didn't like gossip."

She flushed. "I don't."

"Then maybe you should give your sister the benefit of the doubt on all that old stuff." Frowning, he added, "I never believed it for a second."

"You, too?" she demanded in a harsh whisper. "You're going to be on Amanda's side?"

"Not taking sides," he said, pausing for a sip of coffee. "I'm just saying, you're her sister. You should know her better than anyone else and I'm thinking you didn't believe any of that nonsense people were talking about years ago, either."

She flushed again and wasn't happy about JT making her feel guilty. "It's always Amanda," she said bitterly. "Nathan's never looked at me the way he looks at her. How can *anyone* be so blind?"

"Was wondering the same thing myself," JT answered and stood up. He dropped money on the counter and said, "I'll see you tomorrow, Pam."

She watched him go and felt a twinge of regret

for fighting with her best friend, but honestly. Since he *was* her best friend, shouldn't he understand how she felt about all of this? Shouldn't he be on *her* side?

The more she thought about it, the angrier she became, and watching Hannah Poole scurry to yet another table to spread the word about Nathan and Amanda was all the impetus she needed to go and face down her sister.

"What is wrong with you?"

Amanda's sister stormed into the office at the back of the diner a couple of hours later. Morning sunshine streamed through the window and the scent of coffee and fresh cinnamon rolls flavored the air-conditioned air. Amanda sighed and dropped her pen to the desk as the last, lingering effects of early-morning lovemaking disappeared with one look at the woman facing her. Pam's eyes were narrowed, a flush stained her cheeks and her mouth was set in a tight, grim line.

Amanda set aside the paperwork she was laboring over and thought she'd even take a fight with Pam over filling out the supply list for the coming week. She *hated* paperwork and Pam knew it. So, naturally, her sister had completely abdicated that task the minute Amanda came back to town.

She had really hoped that Pam calling and asking for her help meant that her older sister was going to welcome her home. But, if anything, Pam's antagonism seemed fiercer than ever.

Her conversation with Piper ran through Amanda's mind as she looked at Pam, quietly fuming. *Jealousy?* Was it possible? If so, Amanda didn't know how she would fix what was wrong between her and her sister. Because she wasn't about to give up Nathan to make Pam feel better.

"What're you talking about?"

Pam stepped into the office and closed the door quietly behind her with a soft click. Then she leaned against that door, hands behind her back. "You know exactly what I mean, Amanda. The whole town is talking about you. And Nathan."

Her stomach jittered a little, but she'd known going in that she was going to be the hot topic of conversation in Royal. Ever since their dinner out at the TCC, people had been whispering. And

Nathan leaving his car parked outside her place all night had pretty much put the capper on the whole situation.

"I know," she said with a helpless shrug, "but there's nothing I can do about it."

"Well, you could stop chasing after him, that might be a start," Pam snapped, pushing away from the door to stalk to the window overlooking the parking lot behind the diner.

Okay, she was willing to talk. To try to smooth things over with Pam. But she wasn't going to sit there and be attacked without defending herself, either.

"Chasing him?" Amanda stood up. "I'm not chasing Nathan. I've *never* chased him."

Pam whirled around and glared at her, eyes flashing. "Oh, you *love* being able to say that, don't you?"

"What, the truth?"

Pam laughed harshly, walked toward the desk and leaned on the back of the visitor's chair, positioned directly opposite Amanda. Shaking her short hair back from her face, she stared at her sister and blew out a breath before saying, "That just makes it better for you, doesn't it? It's the truth. Nathan chased after you all those years ago and now he's doing it again."

Just for a second, Amanda saw a sheen of tears in her sister's eyes and she felt terrible. Then Pam spoke again and all sympathy went out the window.

"Hannah Poole is sitting out there right now," Pam said, stabbing one finger toward the diner, "telling *everyone* how she saw Nathan's car parked outside your place *all night*."

Amanda winced a little. Well, they'd both known it would happen. They'd just have to ride out the gossip and wait for the first wave to dissipate.

"And this is *my* fault?" Amanda demanded.

"Oh, please." Pam pushed off the chair, making the wooden legs clatter against the linoleum. "Like you don't do everything you can to make sure he notices you. Big eyes. Soft voice."

Amanda laughed shortly. This was getting weird. And how come she had never noticed before just how jealous of her Pam really was? "What are you talking about?"

"When you guys broke up before, it nearly ruined him," Pam told her flatly. She took a deep breath and blew it out again before adding, "He stayed away from Royal for three years. He only saw his brother when Jake went to Dallas to visit him."

They'd both lost a lot, Amanda thought. They had been so young that neither of them had reacted the way they should have to the tragedy that had torn them apart. They'd cut themselves off from not only each other, but also from their friends, their families. It was time they'd never get back, but hopefully, they'd learned something from all of that, too.

But even as she thought it, she wondered if she'd ever really be able to trust Nathan again. He hadn't believed her. Hadn't *loved* her when she had needed him most. Those dark days came back in a rush, swamping her mind with painful shadows until all she could do was whisper, "I stayed away, too, remember?"

Pam waved that off as if Amanda's pain meant nothing. "This was Nathan's home and he didn't come back because he didn't want to deal with having the town gossips tearing him apart. Over *you.*"

And just like that, old pain gave way to fresh anger. Pam was her sister and she was taking Nathan's side in this? *"And?"*

"And now they're doing it again." Pam folded her arms over her chest and tapped the toe of one shoe against the floor. "And just like before, it's all because of you."

In a blink, Amanda's temper ratcheted up to match her sister's. Funny, when they were kids, Amanda had always looked up to Pam. And in an argument, Amanda had always backed down, both intimidated by her sister and unwilling to risk alienating Pam entirely. Well, she thought, those days were long gone. They were both adults now and Pam had been on her case for weeks already. Fine. They had problems—they'd either work them out or not. But damned if Pam was going to wedge herself between Amanda and Nathan.

"This isn't any of your business, Pam. So back off."

Pam drew her head back in surprise. But her

stunned silence only lasted a second or two. "I'm not backing off. I'm the one who's been here, Amanda. I'm the one who saw what you did to Nathan before. And I'm the one telling you to stop ruining his life."

"Ruining his life? A little dramatic, don't you think?"

"Hah. If the gossips chew on him for too long he'll leave again."

"Has it occurred to you that they're gossiping about *me,* too?" She tipped her head to one side, mirrored Pam's stance and waited. She didn't have to wait long.

"That's your own fault," Pam scoffed. "For God's sake, you lured him up to your bed and then were too stupid to tell him to move his car. You *wanted* the whole damn town to see."

"I didn't *trick* him into bed, Pam."

"You didn't have to." Pam blinked frantically to clear away the fresh sheen of tears in her eyes. "All you have to do is be there and he can't see anything else."

Amanda steeled herself against feeling sympathy for her sister. Of course she was sorry to see Pam in pain, but not sorry enough to back away from Nathan so her sister could try to get him. Again. "I still don't see how that's my fault *or* your business."

"Of course you don't," Pam said with an exasperated huff. "It's my business because I care about Nathan. When he came home, I was the one who helped him settle in. He was unhappy for a long time. And, Amanda—" she paused and took a breath "—I just don't want to see him like that again."

That much, Amanda could understand. She didn't want that, either. Because it would mean that whatever was between them had shattered again. Just the thought of that had a cold ball of ice settling in the pit of her stomach. Oh, God, she was never going to get over Nathan. How could she, when she was still in love with him?

Staggered by the sudden acknowledgment of what she was really feeling and worried about what it meant to her present—let alone her future—Amanda plopped down into her desk chair. Love? She hadn't counted on that at all. She'd hoped to make her peace with her memories—not build new ones.

She was in deep trouble. Nausea rolled through her stomach in a thick wave that had her swallowing spasmodically.

"Hey…" Pam's tone changed from banked anger to concern. "Are you okay?"

"No," Amanda told her, and cupped her face in her hands. Oh, God, she was still in love with Nathan. A man she wasn't sure she could trust. She didn't even know how he felt about her! Seven years ago, Nathan had never told her that he loved her. Had left her the moment the reason for marrying her was gone.

Okay, yes, she was the one who had called off the marriage. But he hadn't fought her. He'd simply walked away. As if losing her and their baby meant nothing to him.

Today, there was still no mention of the *L*-word and that hadn't stopped her from once more falling for the only man she would ever love. She'd just tossed her heart into the air not knowing if it was going to crash and burn or find a safe home. "I really don't think I'm okay at all."

"This isn't just a cheap ploy to end the argument, is it?"

On a sardonic laugh, Amanda looked up and met her sister's eyes. "Trust me when I say, I really wish this was a ploy."

# Nine

Summer was rolling along like a runaway freight train. Temperatures were high, tempers were even hotter and Nathan spent most of his time stepping in between arguing parties. Nothing unusual about any of it but for the fact that his head just wasn't in the game.

Hadn't been since that night with Amanda by the river.

Scowling, Nathan was alone in his office, thinking about that morning with Amanda. Waking up in her bed, her body wrapped around his, had eased a sore spot inside him he hadn't even realized was there. Making slow, languid love to her had carried that feeling further, until he was so caught up in her, he'd had to force himself to crawl out of that bed and go to work.

"So much for the plan," he muttered, taking a sip of his coffee.

He guessed it was safe to say his plan was shot. Not only had he not gotten her out of his system, but she was also all he could think about anymore.

It had all seemed so simple. Get Amanda back into his bed and finally get over her. Let go of the past and move the hell on. Instead, she was deeper into his gut than she had been before. Not quite sure how that had happened, Nathan was even less sure about how to reverse the damage already done. Especially when all he wanted to do was make love to her again.

Hell, he was walking around town with a body so hard and tight, it was all he could do to keep from groaning in public. He needed…hell. He just *needed.*

Worse, he didn't want to need Amanda. He wanted to be free of her. Didn't he? Nathan scrubbed one hand across his face and tried to wipe away all of the thoughts clashing together in his mind.

To distract himself, he stared around the inside of his office, letting his gaze sweep across the familiar symbols of the life he'd built for himself in Royal. But none of it brought him the pleasure he usually found in just being there. Until Amanda came back to town, he'd been content. Now, contentment just wasn't enough. He wanted more. Wanted *her.*

The problem was…how to get her.

Oh, sex was great, but that was easy. What he wanted would be more difficult. Hell, he could admit, at least to himself, that he wanted it all. Not just Amanda, but the life they could make together. House. Family. A damn white picket fence.

But he knew the past still loomed between them, a big ugly wall they'd both ignored rather than dealt with.

He leaned back in his chair, kicked his feet to the corner of his desk and crossed them at the ankle. Staring up at the ceiling, he told himself that maybe the past should stay right where it was. Maybe they didn't have to dissect it. Maybe all they had to do was learn from it and let it go.

Trust would be an issue between them for a while, of course, but he could *show* Amanda that he had her back now. Over time, she'd eventually come to believe it.

Nodding to himself, he could see the future play out in his mind. He and Amanda, living in his house on the ranch. Having kids that would play with Jake and Terri's bunch. Long nights and lazy mornings in his bed, wrapped in each other's arms. It was what they should have had years ago.

And what they would have now.

When the door opened, Nathan looked over at the doorway, a scowl on his face.

"Nice welcome," Chance said.

"Sorry. I was doing some thinking." Nathan's feet dropped to the floor, then he stood up and held out a hand to his friend. "What's going on?"

Chance's blond hair looked as though he'd been stabbing nervous fingers through it for hours. His green eyes were troubled and he didn't meet Nathan's gaze directly. Not a good sign.

"Everything okay, Chance?"

"Not really," his friend muttered and rubbed one hand across the back of his neck.

He was backlit by the bright afternoon sunlight and when he turned to close the door, Nathan noticed he locked it, too.

"Okay, what's this about?"

"Nathan, I wouldn't be here if I didn't think you should know about what people are saying."

Instantly, Nathan's back went up and he shook his head. Seven years ago, Chance had been the one to tell Nathan about the rumors spreading. The rumor that Amanda had deliberately ended her pregnancy. Back then, Nathan had been young enough to listen and stupid enough not to question.

Today was different.

"Don't want to hear it," he said and turned his back on Chance to walk to a file cabinet on the far wall.

"Don't you think I know that?" Chance's voice was reluctant but firm. Clearly, he wouldn't be leaving until he'd had his say.

Nathan spun around and said, "I don't give a good damn what people are saying, Chance."

The moment the words left his mouth, he realized they were completely true. Somehow, he just didn't care about being the center of gossip. And damned if he was going to listen to anything people had to say against Amanda. He might make mistakes, but hell if he'd make the *same* ones.

"Well, you'd better listen." Chance glared back at him. "The word is you're not the only guy she's sleeping with. People are saying she's slipping out of town, meeting some other guy. So if she turns up pregnant this time, who's to say you're the father?"

He felt like he'd been punched dead-center in the chest. And for one miserable moment, he let those words slam into his head and heart, too. But they didn't stay because they weren't true and he knew it. Knew it down to his bones. Amanda wasn't a cheat and she wasn't a liar.

His hands curled into fists at his sides and he took one long step toward one of his best friends.

Chance held up both hands and took a step

back. "Hey, I didn't say I believed any of the talk."

"Then why the hell are you telling me this?"

He pushed a hand through his hair. "I didn't want to, but if you want a life with Amanda, then you'd better find out who's spreading the poison and get it stopped."

Chance was right. Years ago, someone had spread lies about Amanda aborting their baby. And yeah, now he could see the lies for what they were. Amanda never would have done that. Back then, he'd been too young and stupid to think past his own fury.

Now things were different.

"On that, we totally agree," Nathan muttered darkly. "I'll find whoever it is and when I do..."

A couple of days later, the diner was packed and Amanda was still reeling from the realization that she was in love. On top of that, her stress level was sky-high just from keeping what she was feeling from Nathan. Then there was the situation with Pam.

She shot a covert look at her sister, ringing up

a customer at the cash register. Things were still strained there, but at least they hadn't argued again.

"Everything okay?"

Amanda turned and forced a smile for Alex Santiago. She refilled his coffee cup, then set the pot down onto the counter.

"Everything's fine," she lied.

He studied her for a moment or two then nodded. "Yeah, I can see that."

"What about you, Alex?" Now that she was looking at him, she noticed that he wasn't giving her one of his million-dollar smiles. His eyes looked shadowed, as if he hadn't been getting much sleep. "Are you all right?"

"I'm fine. Just..." He shrugged and tried, but didn't quite manage to smile at her. "You know how it is. Sometimes, you've got too much to think about."

"That, I understand completely." Whispered conversations from off to her left caught her eye, but Amanda ignored them. If people were going to talk about her, she couldn't stop them.

"I think you do," he said, then took a sip of coffee. "Don't worry about me, Amanda. Everything will be fine."

She might have said something else, tried to draw him out a little if only to erase some of the worry in his eyes, but a shout sounded out.

"Amanda, honey, how long till that burger of mine is ready?" John Davis slapped one meaty hand to his broad chest and gave a groan. "I'm a starvin' man, darlin'."

Alex laughed a little. "Go. Feed the man before he dies of hunger."

She rolled her eyes and patted Alex's hand. "I will. But if you need anything, all you have to do is ask."

He covered her hand with his briefly and said, "You've a kind heart."

Amanda went to pick up John's lunch, then delivered it, all the while wondering about Alex. But by the time she got back to the counter, he was gone. His coffee was still steaming and there was a five-dollar bill next to the saucer. She frowned and looked through the front window in time to see Alex hurry down the street.

* * *

A few days later, Nathan answered the phone at the sheriff's office and smiled. "Alex. What's up?"

"Nothing much," his friend said, then asked, "Are you going to be at the TCC meeting tonight?"

"I'll be there," Nathan said on a tired sigh. "With Beau Hacket still making waves over the child-care center, figured I should attend just to keep him in line."

"That's good," Alex said. "After the meeting, I'd like to talk to you. Privately."

Nathan frowned and straightened up in his desk chair. There was just something about the tone of his friend's voice that set off small alarm bells in Nathan's mind. "Everything all right?"

"Yes," Alex told him quickly. "Absolutely. I'd just like to talk to you."

"Okay, sure." Still frowning, Nathan suggested, "We could grab a late dinner."

"That would be good," Alex said and now relief colored his words. "I'll see you later, then."

"Right." Nathan hung up, but his mind raced with questions.

* * *

That night at the meeting, Nathan wished he could just leave. His heart just wasn't in being there. He'd have much rather been with Amanda.

*What had he come to?* He laughed at himself. Who would have guessed a few weeks ago that he'd be feeling downright…domesticated? He wasn't sure what it was they had going between them, but he was damn sure he didn't want it to end. Was this love? Hell if he knew. He'd imagined himself in love with her seven years ago, but what he felt now was different. Bigger.

He glanced around the meeting room, but didn't make eye contact with any of the people. They were all busy, talking, visiting, but Nathan wasn't in the mood. Hell, he wasn't in the mood for much here lately. Not until he found out who was behind the rumors designed to hurt Amanda.

And, now there was the question of what was bothering Alex, as well. He glanced at the empty chair behind him and wondered again where his friend was. Alex hadn't shown up for the meeting and though Nathan kept telling himself the man would appear at any moment, the meeting was almost over and there was still no sign of him. For the moment, though, he let thoughts of Alex slide away as Amanda's situation took precedence.

From the corners of his eyes, Nathan looked at the familiar faces around him and wondered if it could be one of them. One of his "friends" who had deliberately sabotaged his relationship with Amanda so long ago and was now trying to do the same. But what the hell did anyone have to gain by spreading lies? Not like anyone was going to stop eating at the diner. Or talking to Amanda, for that matter.

So what was the point?

Well now, he thought, he'd know that as soon as he found the bastard.

Raised voices caught his attention and Nathan dragged his thoughts back to the present. Just like every other weekly meeting, there were the same people gathered, having the same arguments. Beau and his bunch were still bitching about the new child-care center and Abby Price looked downright pleased to be able to tell them all to shove off. Couldn't blame her, Nathan thought. She'd fought hard to become a member here at the club. It had to be satisfying to now be able to ensure that not only more women were welcome here, but their kids as well.

Shaking his head, Nathan wondered why Beau couldn't let it go. It was a done deal. Move on.

He caught Chance's eye across the table and the two of them shared a smile.

"I tell you, it's disgraceful," Beau was sputtering. "Putting a babysitting club in the billiards room? Our founding fathers are probably spinning in their graves."

A few raised voices shouted in unison with Beau and the little man seemed to get bigger every time someone sided with him. So before he got out of line entirely, Nathan spoke up.

"No one even *plays* billiards anymore, Beau." The older man was nearly purple in frustrated rage, but Nathan wasn't impressed. He knew Beau was mostly talk. "Hell, when was the last time *you* played the game?"

"Not the point, Nathan Battle, and your own pa would be sore disappointed to hear you taking up on the side of these females." The man wagged a finger at Nathan as if he were a ten-year-old boy.

Chance smothered a laugh and Nathan felt all eyes on him as he said, "That's the thing, Beau. My dad would have been the first one to take a hammer to that moth-eaten old billiards table. And he'd have shamed *you* into giving us a hand remodeling that room for the kids, too."

Beau's color got even worse. His jaw worked and his lips pursed as if there were legions of words trapped inside trying to fight their way out. But he managed to hold on to them and Nathan thought that was probably for the best.

"Now, why don't we end this meeting so we can get on home?" Nathan looked over at Gil Addison, who gave him a wink and a nod before slamming his gavel down with a hard crash.

"Meeting is concluded," Gil announced a second later. "See y'all next week."

Chair legs scraped against the wood floor. Glasses were set onto the table with sharp clicks. Beau was the first one to storm out of the room and once he was gone, conversation picked up as people meandered toward the exit.

"Nice speech," Abby called out as she waved to Nathan.

He smiled and nodded and then turned to Chance when he walked up.

"You shut down Beau pretty well," Chance said.

"Not hard," Nathan answered. "The man's from the Stone Age. Don't know how his wife, Barbara, puts up with him."

"Must have his good points."

"I suppose," Nathan mused, his gaze scanning the TCC members as they filed out, still looking for Alex to come rushing in late. But he didn't show. A trickle of unease rolled along Nathan's spine. He was getting a bad feeling about this—and he'd learned to listen to those bad feelings.

Wasn't like Alex to miss an appointment. In the short time he'd been in Royal, the man had shown himself to be a fiend for schedules. So if he'd wanted to meet with Nathan, where the hell was he?

"Have you seen Alex?" Nathan asked suddenly.

"Not since a day or two ago. Saw him at the diner, talking to Amanda."

People got busy, Nate told himself. Maybe something had come up. But he'd made a point of setting up a private meeting with Nathan. So if he wasn't going to show, why wouldn't he have called to cancel? That bad feeling was getting stronger. He didn't have a concrete reason for it, he supposed, but he couldn't shake that niggling sensation chewing at the back of his mind. Nathan frowned to himself, because he knew a cop had to trust his instincts before anything else. "It's not like him to miss the meeting."

"You know," Chance said, as he also looked around the quickly emptying room, "now that you mention it, I had wondered where he was tonight."

"That's what I'm saying."

Chance shrugged. "Maybe he's on a date or something. Or maybe he just wasn't in the mood to deal with Beau tonight. God knows I wasn't."

"Yeah, but you came anyway," Nathan said firmly. "So would Alex." Especially since he'd wanted to speak privately with Nathan.

"Then where is he?"

"That's the question," Nathan said. "Isn't it? I'll go by his place see what I can find out."

"I've got another question for you." Chance shoved his hands into the pockets of his slacks and started for the door, Nathan walking alongside him. "Discover anything about our gossip starter?"

"No. Not yet." He'd been asking discreet questions all over town, too. Trying to wheedle information out of folks without letting them know that's what he was doing. Most he spoke to were embarrassed to talk to him about the rumors, but they all denied knowing who had started them. It was always, "I heard it from so and so who got it from what's her name." Didn't seem to be a starting point.

But there was one.

And Nathan was going to find it.

"A whole lot of weird going on all of a sudden," Nathan muttered the next morning. "Alex has dropped off the radar and now this at the diner. Doesn't feel like they're connected, but it's damn odd."

"Tell me about it." Amanda's stomach twisted with nerves and knots. "When I got home from your place I went up the back stairs to my apartment and took a shower. I came down after to open up the diner and found this. Then I went to your office to get you."

"Just the right thing," Nathan said as he eased past her in the doorway. "You stay out here, I'll go in and check things out."

"I don't think so," she said and walked into the diner right behind him. "This is my place, Nathan. I'm not waiting outside."

Grimly, he looked at her, mumbled something she didn't quite catch, then said, "Fine. At least stay behind me and don't touch anything."

They walked through the back door directly into the diner kitchen. Amanda looked around the room and still couldn't believe what she was seeing.

The grill was smashed, as if it had been beaten with a hammer. Flour was strewn across everything, making it look like there'd been a snowstorm in the kitchen. Jars of spices lay shattered on the floor, their contents spilled across the flour in festive patterns. Plates were smashed, drawers yanked out and dumped. In essence, the kitchen was a disaster.

"Somebody did a number on this place," Nathan murmured more to himself than to her.

"If I'd been upstairs last night, I would have heard them, damn it." Anger was burning through her nerves.

"Yeah," he said thoughtfully, "you would have. Funny, isn't it, that whoever did this waited until you were spending the night with me on the ranch to do this damage?"

That clicked in immediately. Why hadn't she thought of that? "So who knew I went to the ranch yesterday?" As soon as she asked the question, she sighed in disgust. "Half the town, probably. Everyone saw me leave with you last night."

"Yeah," he said, tipping her chin up so he could look into her eyes. "But not many of them knew you'd be *staying*."

She thought about that for a minute, realized he was right, then tried to make a mental list of who actually knew she'd be gone overnight. "There's

Pam, of course. And Piper. I told her. And Terri." She shook her head, disgusted. "They could have told people, I suppose, but I just can't think of anyone who would do this."

"We'll figure it out." He glanced back at the mess. "I'll have the kitchen fingerprinted, but there are so many people in and out of this diner every day I don't know that we'll find anything."

"No," she grumbled, crossing her arms over her chest. "Probably not. When I first walked in and saw this, I was scared. Now, though, I'm just mad." She kicked at some flour and watched it puff into the air before settling. "This will shut us down for days."

"Might not be too bad," he said. "But you're gonna need a new grill."

She sighed, then tried to look on the bright side. "Well, that grill is older than I am, so maybe we needed a new one anyway. So, once you do your fingerprint thing, I'll call Pam and we'll get this mess cleaned up."

Nathan smiled, shook his head, then grabbed her and pulled her in close for a hug. "You're really something, Amanda Altman."

"Thanks, Sheriff," she said with a smile then sobered. "This is pretty ugly, but I know how concerned you are about Alex. Finding him is important, too."

"Not even really sure why I'm worried," he admitted. "The man could be off taking care of business none of us knew about."

"True," she said, staring up into his eyes. "But you said yourself that he wanted to talk to you about something. Wouldn't he have called to let you know he couldn't make it?"

"Yeah." Frowning, he said, "He would have. You haven't thought of anything else? What he talked about when he was at the diner the other day?"

"No," she said softly. "Ever since you asked me that last night, I've been thinking about it and there's just nothing." Shrugging, she added, "He seemed distracted. Worried about something maybe. But he didn't say anything specific."

He huffed out a breath and shook his head. "Damned strange. All of it."

"I know." She hugged him tightly then let him

go. "I've got a lot of work to do here, Sheriff. So I'll get to it and you go find Alex and catch me a bad guy."

# Ten

Nathan spent a couple of frustrating days trying to track down answers to his questions. He couldn't find Alex Santiago and he had no clue who had vandalized the diner kitchen. Frustration chewed at him. That bad feeling about Alex was intensifying, and as for Amanda…

This was damn personal. Someone was out there trying to hurt her and damned if he'd let them. Amanda was *his* and nobody was going to mess with her and get away with it.

Of course, he mused ruefully, he hadn't told Amanda yet how it was going to be between them. Now that he'd decided that they were going to be together, he wanted to take his time. Keep seducing her with sex, get her used to the idea of having him back in her life before he actually told her it was time to get married. He wasn't an idiot, after all. The last time he'd asked her to marry him it was because of the baby and none of it had ended well. It shamed him to remember it now, but it was best to go into any tricky situation with your thoughts and goals straight. Looking back, Nathan was willing to admit he'd handled that situation badly long ago.

This time would be different.

Amanda was a hell of a woman, but she had a spine and was likely to fight him on this whole marriage thing if he didn't work it just right.

Not that it mattered if she fought him. He would have her, in the end. It would just be easier all the way around if he could just keep reminding himself to be patient.

But he wouldn't be patient in finding whoever was behind this mess at the diner. Because he knew, whoever it was, would also turn out to be the source of the rumors. Highly unlikely that two different people would both be harassing Amanda at the same time.

When the phone rang, he snatched it. "Sheriff's office."

"Hey."

"Chance." Nathan straightened, grabbed a pen and slid a pad of paper in front of him just in case he needed to take notes. "You hear anything?"

"Nada." Chance sounded disgusted. "I've talked to everybody I can think of and nobody's seen Alex."

"Damn." He sat back in his chair and tossed the pen to the desktop. "I talked to Mia Hughes yesterday—Alex's housekeeper. She hasn't seen him in days. Says he hasn't been home at all."

"Well, where the hell is he, then?"

"I don't know, Chance." Nathan shook his head and stared off into space. "It's like he dropped off the face of the earth."

"I don't mind admitting that I'm getting worried, Nate," Chance said. "This isn't like Alex."

Nathan was worried, too. It just didn't seem reasonable that *nobody* in Royal had heard from or seen Alex. And why the hell would he leave town without at least telling Mia? Something was definitely wrong here and Nathan didn't like it.

Usually, in a town like Royal, the "crimes" he dealt with were kids getting into trouble or the occasional battle between neighbors. Now he had a missing man and a break-in.

"Any news on what happened at the diner?" Chance asked.

"No." One word. Disgusted. Nathan had never felt helpless before and he didn't care for it. He couldn't find his friend and he hadn't been able to discover who was behind the vandalism to Amanda's place.

Though he did at least have a half-baked suspicion on that one. Didn't make much sense to him, but he'd check it out. And if he were right… it would help prove to Amanda that she could trust him—in spite of the mistakes in their past.

"What is *with* Royal this summer, man?"

"Wish to hell I knew," Nathan answered.

The upside of having her diner demolished, Amanda thought, was that she had more time with Nathan.

He hadn't wanted her staying alone in the apartment over the diner until he found whoever had done the damage. So, she'd been staying here, at the house he'd had built for himself on the Battlelands. Normally, she might have fought him over his bossy, take-charge attitude, but she hadn't wanted to stay there, either. As much as she liked the little apartment, it would never really feel safe to her again.

Nathan's place, as great as it was, was temporary and she knew it. The only answer was to find a place of her own.

"Guess it's time to look for that house," she said aloud.

"You have a house," Terri told her firmly. "Right here."

"This is Nathan's," Amanda said, shaking her head as she took a sip of her tea. "Being here with him is wonderful, but it isn't permanent."

"Honestly, I don't know which of you has the harder head." As if accepting that she wouldn't change Amanda's mind, Terri sighed and went to a new subject. "How's the diner coming along, anyway?"

"We'll be able to open again on Monday. We've got a new grill and Pam's been helping me clean up and restock the kitchen."

"There's a miracle," Terri murmured. "Pam doesn't exactly strike me as the helpful type."

Amanda had to chuckle. She'd been surprised by her sister's assistance, too. "That's one good thing that came out of all of this. Pam did such a turnaround this last week—she's been so nice it's almost eerie."

"And all it took was the destruction of the diner."

"Whatever caused the change, I'm happy about it." Amanda had never wanted to be at war with her sister. Over the last week, they'd worked together in the kitchen, straightening up, restoring order. Not that she and Pam were joined at the hip or suddenly becoming best buddies…but it was a start. If this new relationship with her sister continued, then the vandalism would have been worth it.

Terri set a paper sack on the kitchen table and pushed it toward Amanda. "I got what you asked for at the store."

Amanda's stomach flip-flopped as she reached for the bag. She took a deep breath then blew it out again. "Thanks, Terri. If I had gone into a store anywhere near here to buy it myself, everyone in town would have known by the end of the day."

"Amanda..."

She cut her friend off. "Remember, you promised. Not a word. Not even to Jake."

Terri made a quick cross over her heart and held her hand up. "I swear. But you're crazy, you know that, right? You should tell Nathan."

"I will," Amanda said. "If there's anything to tell."

"Stubborn," Terri said. "Okay, fine. Do it your way."

"Wow, thanks for that, too," Amanda said with a smile.

"Okay, I'm going. But if you need me, just call. It'll take me a whole ten seconds to walk over here from the main house."

"I'm fine, Terri. But thanks. I appreciate it."

"You're welcome. And I really hope you get

this straightened out already. It'd be nice to have you here on the ranch permanently."

When the kitchen door closed behind her friend, Amanda picked up her tea and the small paper bag and wandered out of the room. Her gaze slipped over Nathan's place and in her mind, she instinctively added pillows, splashes of color, vases filled with summer flowers.

Terri was right about one thing. Amanda didn't want to buy another house. She wanted to live here. With Nathan. But she couldn't do that without love.

Nerves skittered through her already uneasy stomach and Amanda swallowed hard to settle everything down. She'd been here in this house with Nathan for nearly a week and it was becoming too comfortable. Being here with him, having breakfast and dinner together, waking up in his arms—it all felt just right. As it was supposed to have been seven years ago.

But no promises had been made. No talk of a future. No mention of love.

Amanda's heart twisted a little as she reminded herself of that. She couldn't let herself slide into a relationship with Nathan that had no chance of succeeding. And the longer she stayed here with him, the harder it was going to be to leave.

Especially now.

She stopped at a window overlooking the front yard of the main ranch house. Jake and Terri's kids were clambering over the jungle gym Nathan and Jake had built for them. Their shouts and laughter pealed through the morning air and Amanda smiled wistfully as she listened to them.

If things had been different, her child would have been out there with them. *Her child.*

Taking a breath, she turned around and headed for the stairs. She carried her tea up to the master bedroom, sliding her hand along the polished oak banister as she went. Nathan was in town at the sheriff's office. He'd be there for hours.

So, she told herself, there was no better time for her to find out the answer to a question that had been nagging at her for a week.

Pam looked horrible.

It was the first thing Nathan noticed when she opened the front door of her house to him. And that gave Nathan the answer he was looking for. In between his regular town duties and the unofficial search for Alex, Nathan had been working on the vandalism at the diner.

He'd spent hours thinking about this, looking for witnesses, anything to help him figure out who was behind Amanda's troubles. And the one name that kept coming back to him was Pam.

No one else in town had any real issues with Amanda. But her sister hadn't exactly made a secret of the fact that she resented Amanda's presence even though her return to Royal had been at Pam's request. So he was playing a hunch. Trusting his instincts. He'd come to Pam's house to talk to her about this, maybe get her to confess. Now, looking into her eyes, he knew he was right about it all.

"Nathan."

"We need to talk." Nathan walked past her into the darkened house. Drapes were drawn, shutting out the sunlight, as if she were in hiding.

He marched through the small, familiar house and stopped in the living room. Then he snatched off his hat and turned to face the woman following him.

Abruptly, tears filled her eyes and spilled over to run unchecked down her cheeks. “Nathan—”

“You’re sitting here in the dark,” he pointed out. “Looking mighty miserable and I think there’s a reason for that. See, I came here on a hunch,” he said, his voice clipped and hard. “The only person in town who has a problem with Amanda is *you,* Pam. No one else would have had access to the diner without breaking a window or something to get in.” That fact had bothered him from the jump. The lock on the door hadn’t been jimmied, so either he was looking for a skillful vandal with terrific lock-picking talents, or… “But you had a key. You went there in the middle of the night, let yourself in and tore that kitchen apart, didn’t you?”

“I swear I didn’t go there intending to wreck the place,” she murmured, wrapping her arms around herself as if searching for comfort. “I went to get a bottle of wine from the fridge. Then I was there, alone and started thinking about you. And

Amanda. And the more I thought, the angrier I got and before I knew it…"

His stance didn't soften, his voice didn't warm when he said, "Why? Why would you do that to your sister? To your own damn business?"

She unfolded her arms and wiped tears away with both hands before taking a long breath and saying, "I've been so angry for so long."

"Angry about what?" he demanded, his gaze locked on her as if seeing her clearly for the first time. She looked miserable, eyes gleaming with tears, her teeth biting into her lower lip and her shoulders hunched as if she were somehow trying to disappear inside herself.

"You," she admitted finally, staring up at him.

"What the hell are you talking about?"

She laughed harshly. "God, I'm an idiot. Look at you. You have no idea."

"Pam," Nathan growled, "my patience is stretched as thin as it can get. I've had a bad week and I'm not much in the mood for guessing games with you, so whatever's stuck in your craw, spit it out."

"Fine. Why not finish the humiliation?" She

threw her hands high and let them slap down against her sides. Shaking her head, she blurted, "I was always crazy about you, Nathan, but you never looked at me. Never *saw* me."

"Pam—" Nathan said her name and watched her flinch.

She shook her head and held up one hand to keep him quiet. "Please don't say anything. Bad enough I have to say this. Bad enough that I wasted *years* pining after you when I never had a chance." She huffed out a strangled breath. "It was always Amanda for you, wasn't it?"

"Yeah, it was." He didn't feel sorry for her. She'd caused a lot of trouble. He did feel badly that he'd never noticed that her fondness for him had become an obsession. That much was his fault. If he'd been paying attention, he could have spared everyone a lot of misery. As it was, he played another hunch. "What about the rumors attacking Amanda? The ones seven years ago and now? Was that you, too?"

She inhaled sharply and winced as if she were in pain. "Yeah. That was me." She turned away from him as if she couldn't bear to face him.

"God, this is like a nightmare. Even I can't believe what I've done."

"Pam—" He broke off and shook his head. Hard to believe this one woman had caused so much damage. All of it stemming from jealousy. "You spread those lies about Amanda, suggesting she got rid of our baby. And you thought that would make me care for you?"

Her voice dropped to a whisper but in the stillness Nathan heard every word. "I never thought you'd find out."

"And the diner kitchen? What was that about?"

"God. I was in the diner alone." Her strained whisper sounded as if she were having to *push* every word through her throat. "Amanda was spending the night at the ranch. With you. I swear I didn't consciously mean to do all of that. But I picked up an iron skillet and just started beating the grill. I was so angry, so—it doesn't matter," she said brokenly. "It was like I lost my mind for a few minutes. I was so furious with her, for coming home." She looked around at him. "For taking you from me. I just lost it."

He wasn't moved by her confession. If anything, his jaw clenched tighter and his eyes narrowed more. All Nathan could think was that because of Pam, he and Amanda had lost seven years together. "She couldn't take me from you because I was never *with* you."

She dropped into a chair, wrapped her arms around her middle and rocked. "I know. And I'm sorry. I really am. For everything. I wasted so much time. But, Nathan—"

"No, there's no excuse for any of this, Pam," he told her flatly. "And if Amanda wants to press charges against you, I'll throw you into a cell so fast, the world will be a blur."

Her stomach sank. "You're going to tell her?"

"No," he said. "You are."

"Oh, God."

"Yeah," Nathan went on. "See, Amanda's going to marry me as soon as I get around to telling her how things are going to be. And I'm not going to be the one to break the news that her only family betrayed her."

Pam winced at that, but Nathan didn't give a good damn if her feelings were hurt. "Fine," she said. "I'll tell her."

"Do it fast." He stalked out of the house and slammed the door behind him.

Seven years wasted. But it wasn't all Pam's fault and he knew it. As much as he'd like to forget, Nathan had to acknowledge that if he'd had more faith in Amanda and more damn spine, he never would have believed a word of those rumors. Instead, he'd been young enough and stupid enough to let lies throw his life off track.

Well, no more.

Nathan was still fighting off the anger Pam had churned up in him when he parked outside his house. In no mood to talk to Jake, he was glad it was late enough that his brother and his family were already at dinner.

He got out of his car, slammed the door and took a minute to calm himself before going inside to see Amanda. Like he told Pam, he didn't want to be the one to tell her that her own sister had been behind the harassment aimed at her. And if he went in there furious, she'd worm the information out of him whether he wanted to tell her or not.

Still, hard to believe that Pam was the vandal. And the one who'd started all the vicious rumors. But hell, at least he'd solved *one* mystery. Alex's disappearance was still chewing on Nathan. He was making calls, talking to people and, so far, he had nothing. As Alex's friend, Nathan was worried. As a cop, he was frustrated.

Shaking his head, he stared at his house and in spite of everything, the tension inside him easing. Lights were on, and it struck him suddenly that he really liked coming home to this. Always before, he'd leave work and drive up to an empty house, dark windows and a silence that grew thicker with every passing moment. But for the last week, Amanda had been here and she'd etched herself into every damn corner of that house—as well as his heart.

If she left him today—an option that would not be allowed to happen—he still would see her all over his house. He would hear her laugh, catch her scent on every stray breeze, reach for her across his bed.

Even after the rough day he'd had, Nathan smiled as he noted the pots of bright yellow and blue flowers Amanda had set on the porch yesterday. His chest tightened as he recalled her walking along the wraparound porch, muttering to herself about rockers and matching chairs and tables and how nice it would be to sit out on a summer night and watch the moon crawl across the sky.

He wanted that. With her. Wanted to come home to a well-lit house holding the woman he loved. All right, yes, he loved her. He hadn't told her, of course, because their past was still between them and he knew that though she might not admit it, she didn't completely trust him again yet. He couldn't blame her—hell, thinking back about what had happened between them years ago, how they'd ended, made him want to kick his own ass.

But he'd give her everything else. His name. His home. His children. And one day, he'd confess his love and she'd believe him. She'd trust him to not hurt her again as he had before.

He had to have her. Hell, he couldn't draw a breath inside that house without taking the essence of her into his soul. It had always been that way between them. Seven years ago, he'd just been too young to appreciate what he had when he had it. Now he was going to set things right.

Clutching his hat in one fist, he started for the porch. Time to get this done. He'd walk right in there and tell her they were getting married. Amanda was a logical sort of woman. She'd see it was the best plan right off. They'd have a small wedding, here on the ranch. Nathan took the front steps two at a time, a smile on his face.

The front door flew open just as he approached it and Amanda was standing there, staring at him through wide, wonder-filled eyes.

"Amanda?" He stopped dead. "Are you okay?"

"I'm pregnant."

# Eleven

Okay, Amanda thought, she'd had that planned a lot better in her mind. She hadn't meant to just blurt it out like that, but on the other hand, even if she had taken ten or fifteen minutes to tell him, the result would've be the same.

She looked up at him and waited what felt like forever for his reaction. Would he be as happy as she was? Would he be upset? *Say something!*

He scrubbed one hand across his face. "You're what?"

"Pregnant." It felt so good to say. What felt like champagne bubbles were swimming through her system, making her nearly giddy.

"You're sure?"

"Positive." She laughed a little as she'd been doing all afternoon since taking that wonderful little test that Terri had picked up for her. "At least, that's what the test said. Positive."

He shook his head. "How?"

*"Really?"*

He laughed. "That's not what I meant. We used condoms."

"They don't always work, you know." She paused and added, "They didn't work seven years ago, either."

"I remember." He reached out and skimmed his fingers along her cheek.

Memories swirled around them, thickening the air with the haunting ghosts of shattered dreams and broken promises. They'd made an agreement to leave the past behind, but could it ever really be forgotten? Weren't you supposed to not dismiss your past, but learn from it?

Well, Amanda had. She'd lived through the pain, built a life, grown and changed. But the dreams of her heart were still there. Nathan. A family. She caught his hand in hers and held tight.

Amanda had had a couple of hours to get used to this news and she figured it would take Nathan at least a few minutes to do the same. She wanted him to be happy about it, but the honest truth was, even if he didn't want the baby, *she* did.

Seven years ago, she'd been young and scared and too unsure about her own future to feel capable of raising a child on her own. But she was different now.

She had a home. A job. A place in this town. And if she had to, she would gladly raise this baby as a single mom. It was as if she'd been given a second chance to have all of the dreams she'd been denied so many years ago.

"This is…" He drew her into the house and closed the door. Tossing his hat onto the nearest chair, he laughed again. "This is *great.*"

Relief and joy swept through Amanda on a tide so high and wide, she could barely breathe through the richness of it. "You're happy about the baby?"

"Happy?" Nathan laughed, reached out, grabbed her and swung her in a circle before finally setting her on her feet and pulling her in close.

"Amanda, it's like we've got a second chance, here."

"That's just what I was thinking," she agreed, wrapping her arms around his waist and holding on. She leaned her head on his chest and listened to his galloping heartbeat.

"We can get married here at the ranch," he said. "Actually, I was planning for us to be married, anyway."

She went still, then drew her head back and looked up at him. "I'm sorry. You were planning for us to be married?"

"Yeah. I was going to tell you about it tonight." He grinned at her. "But your news kind of threw my plan off."

"Your plan." A trickle of cold began to seep through the happy glow she'd been carrying inside.

He gave her a hard hug. "I figured we could get married here at the ranch."

"Did you?" The cold went a bit deeper now, but she steeled herself against it.

The past seemed suddenly so much closer. She was reliving it all. His announcement that they would be married. The baby she carried. Would she also relive the shattered dreams?

Nathan frowned a little. "We don't have to hold the ceremony at the ranch, but I thought it'd be easier. Terri will help you set everything up. I'll help when I can, but I'm still looking for Alex and—"

He had it all worked out. And with every word he spoke, her heart sank a little bit more. The buzz of excitement and joy she'd felt earlier was quickly being swamped by feelings of disappointment and, okay, yes, irritation. She couldn't believe this. Although, it was so typical of Nathan, she really should have expected it. Seven years ago, he'd done the same and she'd allowed it because she had wanted him badly enough to hope that one day he might tell her he loved her. Now, though, she wouldn't settle. Slipping out of his arms, she took a step away from him, folded her arms over her chest and stared at the man who had held her heart since she was a kid.

How could she be so dispirited and so in love with him at the same time? Had to be a sort of cosmic joke on her that the one man who could drive her to distraction was the only man she'd ever wanted.

"So you've got everything figured out, have you?" Amanda asked, her voice soft and cool.

"Not completely," he admitted. "But between the two of us it shouldn't take long."

"You're right about that," Amanda said, shaking her head as she looked up at him. "Won't take long at all, since I'm not going to marry you."

"Of course we're getting married."

"Nothing's changed, has it?" she asked, not really expecting a response. "Seven years ago, you decided we'd get married and I went along." He opened his mouth to speak, but she continued quickly. "But I'm not a kid anymore, Nathan. I make my own choices. My own decisions. I won't let you push me into a marriage you don't really want."

"What're you talking about?" He looked as astonished as he sounded.

"What I'm saying is, this is just like before. You're offering marriage because I'm pregnant. Because it's the *right* thing to do." She turned abruptly and walked away from him, into the living room. He was right behind her.

The huge room boasted views of the ranch from every window. Across the drive, the main ranch house was brilliantly lit and Amanda knew that inside, Terri and her family were cozy and happy. Envy curled inside her and twisted around her heart like tangled ribbons. She'd like that for herself. For her child. But she wasn't going to make the same mistakes she'd made seven years ago. She wouldn't be a duty. She wouldn't be a problem that Nathan felt honor bound to clean up.

"It's the right thing to do because we belong together," Nathan argued.

"Do we?" She didn't know anymore. She'd always believed it, but she'd been shot down before and now, if she went along with Nathan's plan she'd only be setting herself up for a possible repeat of history.

"I think we should talk this through," he said.

She shook her head, never taking her gaze from the scene sprawling outside the window. She would miss it here, but it was definitely time to leave. Glancing over her shoulder at him, she said, “I don’t think so, Nathan.”

He was looking at her as if she’d sprouted another head. She could almost smile about that. Nathan was so used to being obeyed, he didn’t know what to do when someone simply said no.

So she took a breath and tried to explain. “Nathan, I know this is just instinct to you. To do the right thing. The honorable thing.”

“And that’s *bad?*”

“Of course it’s not bad,” she countered, and gave him a sad smile. “But it’s no reason to get married. I went along with your demands last time because, frankly, I was too scared to have a baby on my own. But I’ve changed, Nathan. And I’m not going to be just another duty to a man with too much honor. I want to be loved Nathan, or I’m not going to get married at all.”

He threw up his hands. “But I *do* love you.”

Pain sliced at her. If he’d led with that, maybe things would be different right now. But he hadn’t mentioned anything about love until he absolutely *had* to, so how could she trust it? How could she believe anything but that Nathan would use whatever he had to to win.

"I wish I could believe that," she said after a long moment. "I really do."

"Why the hell can't you?" he argued. "Is it so impossible to believe?"

"Yeah, it is," she said and moved farther away. God, she couldn't stay here. Couldn't be this close to him, knowing that she couldn't have him. She needed to be home. Back in the tiny, hot box of an apartment over the diner. She needed to think.

"Amanda," he said, stepping closer, keeping his gaze locked with hers. "You can believe me. I do love you."

"No, you don't," she said, shaking her head as she backed up toward the chair where she'd dropped her purse earlier. "You just want me to fall in line and you know this is the way to manage it. No. It's just a little too convenient, don't you think? I say I won't get married without love and boom. Suddenly you love me? I don't think so."

"It's not suddenly," he argued. "I've loved you most of my life."

That stopped her for a second as his words ricocheted around inside her, tearing at her heart. She wanted to believe, she really did, for both her own sake *and* the baby's. But how could she? And if she took a chance—trusted him with her heart—and was wrong…then it wasn't only she who would pay the price. She had her child to think about now.

"Why is it, then, that you've never mentioned it before now, Nathan?" she asked quietly, sadly.

"I don't know," he muttered, shoving one hand through his hair.

She picked up her purse and rummaged one hand inside for her car keys. When she found them, she curled her fingers around them and said, "Until you know the answer to that, Nathan, there's nothing else to talk about. Now, I'm going home."

"You are home, Amanda."

That little arrow scored a direct hit on her heart. She had hoped this would be home. Had imagined it. But she couldn't have what she wanted—without first having what she needed. Amanda needed to be loved by the very man standing there giving her all the right words without the meaning.

"No, I'm really not." She shook her head and walked past him. He stopped her with a hand on her arm.

"Don't go."

She looked down at his hand then shifted her gaze to his eyes. "I have to."

He released her then and Amanda felt the loss of his touch all the way to her bones. It took everything she had to walk out the door and down the front steps. Before she reached her car, she looked back over her shoulder and Nathan was standing there, in the open doorway, watching her.

"This isn't over," he said, his deep voice carrying on the warm summer air.

Amanda knew that all too well. What she felt for Nathan would *never* be over.

"Anyway," Pam said later that evening. "What I'm trying to say is, I'm sorry."

What a day this had been, Amanda thought, staring at her sister in dumbfounded shock. A surprise pregnancy, a surprise proposal and now…a sister who had hated her enough to try and ruin her life. Her heart hurt at the realization that Pam had been behind the rumors that had torn Amanda and Nathan apart so long ago. But a voice in her mind whispered that Nathan shouldn't have believed those rumors. He should have loved her enough to know they weren't true.

And he hadn't.

"You're sorry." Amanda whispered the words and watched Pam flinch. "For all the rumors or for the diner?"

"Both." Pam dropped into a chair beside the sofa where Amanda was curled up.

The diner apartment was too warm, the air conditioner wasn't working again. Amanda reached for her glass of iced tea and took a long drink as she studied her sister. Pam looked awful. Her eyes were red and puffy from crying. Her hair was in a tangle as if she'd forgotten to brush it and misery pumped off of her in waves.

Right now, Amanda told herself, she should be furious. Should be raging at her sister for all the damage Pam had done over the years. But the bottom line was, Amanda's heart was already too broken to break again. And fury seemed to require more effort than she had the energy for at the moment.

"God," Pam said softly, "I was always so jealous of you."

"Why?" Amanda shook her head and stared at her. "You're my big sister, Pam. I always looked up to you."

Pam winced. "And I resented you. You were always the favorite. With Mom and Dad, with our teachers at school. With Nathan."

"I don't even know what I'm supposed to say to that," Amanda said quietly. "Mom and Dad loved us both and you know it."

"Of course they did, and I'm an idiot for clinging to all that junk from when we were kids and letting it chew on me until I lost it."

"Pam…"

"There's nothing you have to say. It was all me, Mandy," Pam whispered, unconsciously using the name Amanda hadn't heard since she was a little girl. "I got so twisted up inside, I couldn't see anything but my jealousy of you. And even if you don't believe me, I am really sorry."

"I do believe you." Funny. She could accept Pam's apology but she couldn't trust Nathan's proclamation of love. A very weird day.

Pam looked at her from where she was sprawled in the overstuffed, faded chair. "You do?"

"Yeah." She shook her head tiredly. "Not that it's okay with me, what you did. And we're going to have to talk about this more, figure out where we go from here, but you're still my sister…." Heck, Amanda understood better than anyone what it was to be so crazy about Nathan that you could lose yourself in the emotional pool. And, there was the fact that Amanda was going to need her sister in the coming months. She could raise a child alone, but she wanted her baby to have a family. An aunt to love him or her.

Pam drew a deep breath and let it out on a relieved sigh. Her lips curved in a tired smile that looked quivery at the edges. "I didn't expect you to forgive me so easily."

Amanda tried to find a return smile, but

couldn't. "I didn't say it would be easy. You're paying for the damage to the diner."

"Agreed," Pam said.

"And," Amanda continued, since she had her sister at a disadvantage at the moment, "you're taking over the paperwork again."

Pam nodded. "I only dumped it on you because you hate it. I actually sort of like it. I was always good with numbers."

"I know, I used to envy that," Amanda mused, realizing that for the first time in years, she and her sister were having a real conversation. "Maybe you should think about going back to school. Getting an accounting degree."

Pam thought about that for a second and then smiled. "Maybe I will." She pushed her hair back behind her ears. "Gotta say, Amanda, you've been a lot nicer to me about this than I deserve."

"You know," Amanda said thoughtfully, "you're lucky you picked today to dump all of this on me."

"Why?"

Amanda frowned and tapped her fingernails against the glass she held. "Because I'm too tired from dealing with Nathan at the moment to work up any real rage for you."

"I'm so sorry, Amanda," Pam said again. "I know you and Nathan were having a hard time and I didn't make it any easier. But he made it clear today that you two were getting married and—"

Amanda went still as stone. "He what?"

Pam shrugged. "He said you would be marrying him as soon as he told you his plan and—"

"He told you he was going to marry me even before he bothered to mention it to *me?*"

"Yeah, apparently."

There was a part of Amanda that was excited to hear it. After all, he'd seen Pam *before* he knew about the baby. So he had planned to propose anyway—that was something. It didn't change the fact that he'd mentioned nothing about love, though, until he was forced to by the situation.

"Well," she murmured, "it doesn't change anything. I already told him I'm not going to marry him just because he decrees it to be so."

"You said no?" Incredulous, Pam's voice went high.

"Of course I said no. I'm not going to agree to marry him just because I'm pregnant again."

"You're pregnant?"

Amanda wrapped her arms around her middle as if giving her unborn child a comforting hug. "I am, and I can raise *my* baby all by myself. The baby will have a mom and an aunt, right?"

Smiling, Pam said, "Absolutely. Aunt Pam."

Amanda nodded. "I can do this and I can do it without Nathan Battle if I have to."

"If he lets you," Pam muttered.

"Lets me?" Amanda repeated, staring at her sister. "Did you just say if he *lets* me?"

Pam lifted both hands. "You know Nathan. He doesn't usually hear the word 'no.'"

"Well, he'll have to hear it this time. I'm going to live my life my way. I'm not going to be told what to do and where to go and who to love." She walked over to the window and stared down at Royal. It was dark and streetlights created puddles of gold up and down the street. Overhead, the moon hung like a lopsided teeter-totter and the stars winked down on the world.

And over on the Battlelands, the man she loved was alone with his *plans.* She hoped he was as lonely as she was.

"Sure am glad the diner's back open."

It was a couple of days later when Hank Bristow lifted a cup of coffee and took a long, leisurely sip. He sighed in pure pleasure before picking up his coffee and heading for a group of his friends at a far table. "Didn't know what to do with myself when you girls were closed."

"We're glad to be open again, too, Hank," Amanda assured him as he walked away.

She glanced at her sister. Pam was like a different person. The old bitterness was gone and she and Amanda had spent the last couple of days building a shaky bridge between them. Someday, Amanda hoped the two of them would be close. It wouldn't happen overnight, of course, but at least now there was a chance that the Altman girls were finally going to have a good relationship.

"Earth to Amanda…"

She jolted a little and, laughing, turned to look

at Piper, sitting on a stool at the counter. "Sorry. Mind wandering."

"It's okay, but since I'm starving, how about a doughnut to go with this excellent coffee?"

"You bet." It was good to have friends, Amanda thought as she opened the door to the glass display case and set a doughnut on a plate. Piper had been the one Amanda went to after Nathan's abrupt proposal. And Piper was the one who had insisted that Nathan *did* love Amanda, that he was just being male and sometimes that had to be overlooked.

Amanda wasn't so sure. She'd missed Nathan desperately the last couple of days. He hadn't called. Hadn't come to her. Was he waiting for *her* to go to *him?* How could she?

She set the doughnut in front of Piper and whispered, "Thanks again for everything."

"No problem," Piper told her and took a sip of coffee. "I'm guessing you still haven't heard from him."

"No." Amanda planted both hands on the counter. "I don't think I will, either. Nathan's a proud man—maybe *too* proud. And I turned him down and walked away."

"Then maybe you should go to him," Piper said matter-of-factly.

"How can I?" Amanda shook her head.

"Give him a chance, Amanda. Heck, everyone in town knows Nathan's crazy about you. Why can't *you* believe it?"

She wanted to. More than anything.

Walking along the length of the counter, Pam refilled coffee cups, chatted with customers and stopped when she reached JT in his usual spot. "More coffee?"

"Thanks." He watched her in silence for a second, then said, "Looks like you and Amanda got things sorted out."

She set the coffeepot down and glanced at her sister. "We're getting there. I guess you could say I finally grew up."

All around them, the diner was buzzing with morning conversations, so JT's words were almost lost in the sound when he said, "It's about time."

Pam smiled. "True enough. JT, why are you always so nice to me?"

In answer, he stood up and came around the end of the counter. When he was close enough, he grabbed hold of Pam, pulled her in tight, then bent her over in a dip as he kissed her, long and slow. Finally, he swung her back onto her feet and let her go.

"*That's* why," he said, grinning at her. "Any other questions?"

The whole diner was silent as everyone in the place focused on the drama playing out right in front of them. A second ticked past, then two. Pam lifted one hand and rubbed her fingertips across her lips, then grinned widely. "Only one question, JT McKenna. What in hell took you so long?"

Applause burst into the room as Pam leapt into JT's arms and kissed him back.

The rest of the day passed quickly as people came and went, and life in Royal marched on. Amanda did her work, smiled and talked with her customers all while trying to breathe past the knot in her throat. Thoughts of Nathan crowded her mind and the emptiness she felt without him left an ache in the center of her chest.

JT had taken up permanent roost at the end of the counter and Pam took every chance she could to stop for a kiss as she passed him. A patient man, JT had waited years for Pam to finally realize that *he* was the man for her.

Nathan wasn't patient, Amanda told herself. He didn't wait. He pushed. He nudged. He ordered and when that didn't work, just went ahead and did whatever he thought was the right thing to do.

As those thoughts wandered through her mind, Amanda realized that she'd always known that about Nathan. And she loved him for who he was, irritations and all. So how could she blame him for doing everything he could now to make sure she married him?

Sighing, she glanced out the front window toward Main Street and her breath caught when she saw Nathan headed for the diner. Just one look at him and her heartbeat jumped into a gallop. He had his hat pulled down low against the brilliant summer sunshine and his steps were long and determined. She could almost feel the intensity preceding him as he stalked ever closer, people instinctively moving out of his way.

Amanda fought for calm and didn't find it. Her heartbeat continued to race and her stomach swirled with expectation.

He stepped into the diner and his gaze swept the place in seconds, finally landing on her as if drawn to her by some immutable force. She felt the power of his stare from across the room and couldn't look away from those dark brown eyes that were filled with heat and charged with emotion.

The crowd in the diner took a collective breath and held it. Excitement fluttered through the room as people shifted positions to get a good view of whatever was coming next. Amanda didn't care. She wasn't thinking about anything but Nathan and why he'd come. If he was just here for more of the same, she'd have to tell him no and send him away again, though the thought of that tore at her.

Yes, he was arrogant and pushy and bossy and proud and she loved him desperately.

"Amanda," he announced, loud enough for everyone to hear, "I've got a few things to say to you."

"Here?" she asked. "In front of half the town?"

"Right here, right now," he told her, and his gaze bored into hers. "We've been trying to outrun or hide from gossip and rumor for so long… I think it's time we just took a stand." He moved a bit closer to her and his voice dropped a notch or two. "I don't care what they think. What they say. Let 'em look, Amanda. We're done hiding."

A flush of heat swamped her, but she found herself nodding in agreement. He was right. They had worried over rumors. They'd allowed vicious lies to split them up seven years ago. Maybe it was time to just be themselves without worrying over what the rest of the town had to say about it.

"You're right," she said. "No more hiding."

One corner of his mouth lifted into a brief half smile and she saw pride glittering in his eyes. For a second or two, the terrible tension in her chest eased and Amanda felt as if she and Nathan were a team. The two of them against the gossips.

Close enough to touch her now, he started talking. "I thought a lot about what we talked about the other night."

His voice was low and deep and seemed to reverberate up and down her spine. His eyes were locked on hers and she couldn't have looked away if she'd tried.

Reaching out, he stroked his fingertips along her cheek and Amanda shivered, closing her eyes briefly to revel in the sensation of his touch. When she opened her eyes again, he was still watching her.

"You were right, Amanda," he said. "The night you told me about the baby, I said the words you needed to hear to help convince you to marry me."

It felt as if all the air slid from her lungs at once. The tightness in her chest was painful and tears pooled at the backs of her eyes.

"But—" He cupped her face in his palms, and held her, forcing her to keep looking into his eyes. "That doesn't mean they weren't true."

"Nathan—" She shook her head and tried to look away. He wouldn't allow it.

"I do love you. I always have." He bent and

kissed her gently on the lips and the taste of him lingered on her mouth. "Maybe telling you when I did was bad timing."

"Maybe?" she managed to ask.

He gave her a nod and a rueful smile. "You threw me that night, Amanda, but I *do* love you, with everything in me. If I hadn't been too young and too arrogant to say the words seven years ago…maybe things would have been different for us."

Amanda knew the whole diner was listening in and found she didn't care. The only person she was interested in now was Nathan. "I want to believe you," she said. "I really do."

"You *can,*" he told her, moving into her, until every breath she took drew the clean, fresh scent of him deep into her lungs. "We're meant to be together, and I think you know it."

He reached into his pocket and pulled out a small, red velvet jeweler's box. Her gaze landed on it even as her heart took another tumble in her chest. When she looked up at him again, he smiled.

"This is for you, Amanda."

She shook her head even as he opened the lid to display a brilliant topaz stone surrounded by diamonds and set in a wide, gold band.

"This stone is sort of the color of your eyes," he whispered, "at least, *I* think so. Every time I look in your eyes, I fall in love again. You're the woman for me, Amanda. The *only* woman. So I'm asking you now. The right way. Amanda Altman, will you marry me?"

She shook her head and blinked to clear away the tears blurring her vision. He was offering her everything she'd ever wanted. Love. The promise of a future together. All she had to do was trust her heart and take a leap of faith.

She looked away from the ring and into his eyes and nearly cried again when she read in his eyes the truth she'd needed so much to see. Warmth, passion, *love*.

Before she could say anything, Nathan continued. "When you left the other night, you took my heart with you," he said, gaze moving over her face like a caress. "I couldn't breathe. Couldn't sleep. Couldn't do anything but try to think of a way to bring you back home where you belong."

"Oh, Nathan." The diner, their audience, the whole world fell away and all that was left was the two of them. She and Nathan, together as she'd always dreamed they would be.

"I let you go once," he said tightly. "I don't know how I lived these years without you, but I *know* I can't live the rest of my life without you."

Her tears overflowed and tracked along her cheeks unheeded. Gently, he used his thumb to wipe the tears away and gave her a sad smile.

"I was young and stupid seven years ago," Nathan said, "but I've changed as much as you have. I know you could raise our child on your own—but I hope you won't." He took the ring from the box and slowly, carefully, slid it onto her ring finger, then kissed it as if to seal the ring in place. When he looked into her eyes again, he said, "I want to be with you, Amanda. Always. I need you. And our baby. And the family we'll build together. The family we should have started all those years ago."

She couldn't look away from his eyes and, in truth, she didn't want to. The ring felt warm on her hand and her heart felt even warmer. Amanda took a breath and slowly let it out, enjoying this moment, wanting to treasure the memory of this one small slice of time forever.

This was everything she'd ever wanted. He was saying the words that were so important to her. Offering her the life she craved. And she believed him. Nathan's eyes were filled with love as he looked at her and she knew that she would never doubt him again.

All around her, she sensed people's attention, knew they were all listening in and found she simply didn't care.

"I love you, too, Nathan," she said and smiled when he grinned down at her. "I just needed to believe."

"And now you do?" he asked, wrapping one arm around her waist to hold her to him.

"Now I do," she said and realized she'd never been more sure of anything than she was of what she and Nathan shared. For a while, she had allowed doubts and fears from the past to cast dark shadows over the present and the future. But she was through looking backward.

"I swear, you'll never be sorry." He swept her up

tightly to him and kissed her so deeply, Amanda would never again have any doubts about his feelings.

And while the people in the diner broke into applause, Amanda knew that she finally had everything she had ever wanted.

The man she loved, loved her back, and there was nothing in the world more beautiful than that.

# Epilogue

The wedding wasn't as small as Nathan wanted and not as large as Amanda had feared.

There was family—Jake, Terri and the kids. Pam and JT, practically joined at the hip. Amanda had the distinct feeling it wouldn't be too long before there was another wedding in Royal.

And there were friends. Piper and Chance and Abby and so many others gathered together to wish them well.

Nathan had surprised her by outfitting the wraparound porch of their home with all of the rockers and gliders and chairs that she'd talked about once. She could see them in the years to come, sitting on that porch, surrounded by family, and it filled her heart to the point of bursting.

To avoid the steaming heat of a Texas summer, on the last day of July, the wedding was held in the evening. Lanterns were strewn across the yard, lending a soft glow that was matched only by the early starlight. Flowers in vases, wreaths and vines trailed from every available surface and sweetened the air with a perfume that flavored every breath.

Tables groaned with food and music played from the stereo situated on Jake's front porch. Children clambered all over the swing set Jake and Nathan had built while their parents chatted with friends. There was laughter and there was *love.*

Amazing how love, when it finally arrived, made the whole world shinier, brighter, more filled with promise.

"A bride as beautiful as you are shouldn't be standing here alone," Nathan said as he came up behind her and wrapped his arms around her waist.

She leaned back into him and smiled, loving

the feel of him pressed close, knowing, *trusting* now, that he always would be. "I was just thinking how perfect today was."

"Agreed," he said and dipped his head to kiss her cheek. "The only way it could have been better was if Alex were here, too."

Amanda turned in his arms and looked up at him. She knew his friend's disappearance was haunting Nathan. It had been nearly a month now and there were just no clues to follow. "You'll find him, Nathan. And everything will be okay."

He nodded, glanced out over the crowd gathered at the Battlelands, then turned his gaze back to hers. "I'm going to have to officially declare him missing."

A twinge of worry caught her, but she let it go again because of her faith in Nathan. He would find a way to make this right. "You'll find him."

"I will," he said, then smiled. "But that's for tomorrow. Today is for dancing in the moonlight with the woman I love."

"I'm never going to get tired of hearing that, you know."

He led her onto the makeshift dance floor installed on the front yard specifically for the wedding. And as they moved to the music and their friends and family applauded, Nathan promised, “I’m never going to stop saying it.”

Amanda gave herself up to the moment, to the magic, to the man who would always be the very beat of her heart.

* * * * *